PENGUIN BOOKS

AFTER HENRY

Simon Brett was born in 1945 and educated at Dulwich College and Wadham College, Oxford. Apart from a brief spell as Father Christmas in a department store, he has worked for BBC Radio and London Weekend Television, where he was Producer of Light Entertainment from 1977 until 1979. Since then he has been a full-time writer. He is the author of fifteen highly acclaimed crime novels and various humorous books, has edited three Faber anthologies and has written prolifically for television and radio. His work has been translated into fourteen languages.

Simon Brett is married with three children and lives in Sussex.

D0878105

SIMON BRETT

AFTER HENRY

PENGUIN BOOKS

PENGUIN BOOKS

Published by the Penguin Group
27 Wrights Lane, London w8 5TZ, England
Viking Penguin Inc., 40 West 23rd Street, New York, New York 10010, USA
Penguin Books Australia Ltd, Ringwood, Victoria, Australia
Penguin Books Canada Ltd, 2801 John Street, Markham, Ontario, Canada L3R 1B4
Penguin Books (NZ) Ltd, 182–190 Wairau Road, Auckland 10, New Zealand

Penguin Books Ltd, Registered Offices: Harmondsworth, Middlesex, England

First published by Viking 1987
Published in Penguin Books 1988

Made and printed in Great Britain by
Richard Clay Ltd, Bungay, Suffolk
Filmset in Lasercomp Sabon

To Pete Atkin,
who got the whole thing started,
with thanks

Contents

Chapter 1

The Older Man

The only thing wrong with Dr Henry France was that he was dead. At the age of forty-six, he had been killed in a car crash. And, although no blame for the accident could be attributed to him, his death did cause problems. Three problems, really. His wife Sarah, his daughter Clare and his mother-in-law Eleanor. Three women. All living in the same house when he died. And two years later, all still living in the same house. After Henry.

Very few people die at the right time, but it often seemed to Sarah France – as it does to many widows – that her husband's death could not have come at a worse moment. The family had moved less than a year before from London to a quieter practice in a country town some seventy miles from the capital. They had bought an ample Edwardian family house, with three floors and a basement, and Sarah, already slightly bemused by the realization that she had imperceptibly reached forty, was still adjusting to the culture shock of country life.

Her daughter Clare was at that stage of adolescence when disarming babyishness alternated rapidly with truculence and slamming doors.

And – perhaps most difficult from Sarah's point of view – Eleanor Prescott had moved into the flat upstairs.

Sarah's mother had been widowed some three years before the move from London, and it had been Henry France who, with typical magnanimity, had suggested her living under the same roof as the rest of the family. Sarah had had misgivings from the start, but these had been breezed away by Henry's customary charm. 'Don't worry, she'll have a separate entrance. Be able to live an independent life. We'll hardly see her. Come on, Sarah, between the two of us, we can cope with your mother.'

And between the two of them, they could. But, with Henry suddenly removed from the scene, Sarah didn't find coping so easy.

It was not that she did not love her mother, but, as in many family relationships, the love was so coloured by memories of past conflicts, blackmails and compromises that, to the casual observer, it could at times be mistaken for some other, less respectable, emotion.

So for two years, what with curbing her mother's natural instinct to take over everything, and tiptoeing through the minefield of her daughter's adolescence, while at the same time trying to reassemble some kind of new life for herself from the fragments into which Henry's death had broken her old one, Sarah France had had her work cut out.

But, even though it didn't help in her lowest moments of self-doubt and loneliness, she could recognize that she was better off than many widows. For a start, she was better off financially. Her husband's pension provisions, though not lavish, gave her a cushion against total penury.

And also, thank God, she had a job. Working in and a second-hand bookshop. Not perhaps a great job in terms of career or income, but a great job in that it involved daily contact with the bookshop's owner. Gently gay and incurably curious, her boss Russell offered to Sarah that blessing which so few widows are lucky enough to possess – someone to talk to.

In the two years since Henry's death, certain family rituals had changed and others vanished. Some had vanished leaving no trace, others left voids of pain that could never be ignored. One such was breakfast time. Every morning, for the twenty-one years of their marriage, Sarah France had cooked Henry the large breakfast which he needed to keep him going through the gastronomically unpredictable day of a GP. And this chore, so often resented while obligatory, was now one of those rituals whose absence caused a daily pang.

But things moved on, and a new morning ritual had now established itself. This involved Sarah trying to make Clare have a proper breakfast, and Clare trying to gulp a cup of coffee and be out of the kitchen before her mother came downstairs.

On this particular morning, one of those September days whose over-hearty brightness is a reminder of winter's approach, Clare wasn't quick enough. Sarah opened the kitchen door and discovered her daughter, dressed in the neat blue suit she would wear to her work at the local building society, standing guiltily by the draining-board, a coffee cup at her lips.

Sarah tightened her dressing-gown belt firmly round her waist. 'Morning. Have you had breakfast?'

'Um . . .'

It was tantamount to an admission. Sarah crossed to open the fridge, and took out a plate of bacon rashers.

'You must have some breakfast.'

'Why?'

The eternal question. Sarah wondered how many times, from the age of two onwards, Clare had asked that. It must stretch into millions.

'I don't like breakfast,' her daughter continued.

'You need it. You're growing,' Sarah asserted automatically.

'I hope I'm not. I've done quite enough growing, thank you. I don't want to grow any more.'

A sudden panic, born of reading too many Sunday newspaper features, struck Sarah. 'You're not anorexic, are you?'

But a glance at Clare, who had exchanged puppy fat for womanly contours without noticeable loss of weight, showed up the fatuousness of the question.

Clare didn't even bother to answer it. 'Listen, Mummy, I am eighteen, quite old enough to know that I don't like breakfast. All I want in the morning is a cup of coffee.'

'It's not enough for you. You really ought to –'

'You only ever have coffee,' Clare accused.

Wearily Sarah put the plate of bacon down on the kitchen table. Back to the other eternal question of childhood. Why should I have to do something when you don't? Sarah didn't think she'd achieve much with the old 'Do what I say, not what I do' argument, so she fell back feebly on, 'Yes, but that's different.'

This was rewarded by another, predictable 'Why?'

'It's a logical decision that I have reached. I have come to realize that my metabolism doesn't need anything to eat in the morning.'

'Exactly what I have come to realize.' Clare gave a little triumphant grin. 'Hereditary metabolism.'

4

'But I didn't realize it till I was twenty.'

Her daughter shrugged. 'So you were a slow developer.'

'No, I –'

Clare pressed home her advantage. 'You didn't realize it until you left home, until you got away from Granny. I bet she used to force you to have a cooked breakfast every morning.'

'Yes, she did, but –'

'Exactly as you are forcing me.'

Sarah had to admit a logical defeat. She turned away to switch on the coffee-machine, as Clare continued.

'So let's just forget it, shall we? Cut breakfast out of the day. I mean, it made some sense while Daddy was alive . . .'

Sarah was obscurely pleased by the reference. Clare usually clammed up to the point of not mentioning her father; for her to bring his name up, in any context, seemed a kind of advance.

'Yes,' said Sarah, in a voice that she hoped didn't sound wistful, 'Henry liked his breakfast.'

'But you don't and I don't, so don't let's pretend. Forget it.'

'But –'

'And, while we're at it, let's forget talking to each other in the morning as well.'

'Clare!'

'I think that talking to anyone before 9 a.m. is an unnatural act and should be punishable by law.'

Sarah started to protest, but was overruled.

'Go on, Mummy, you agree. We're both dreadful in the mornings. Same metabolism again.'

It was very difficult, Sarah was finding, to conduct an argument when she agreed with most of what her opponent was saying. She grinned. This sparring with Clare was not an unhealthy symptom in their relationship. It was a kind of communication; better at least than when her daughter went silent on her.

But Sarah's momentary comfort was briskly removed by Clare taking a final gulp of her coffee and announcing, 'Never mind. It'll all be simpler when I move out.'

Her mother could only echo, 'When you move out?'

'Yes. Into a flat.'

'You're planning to move into a flat?'

'Yes.' Clare swilled the dregs of her coffee into the sink and placed the cup firmly on the draining-board. 'I must go,' she said, sweeping across the kitchen.

'But, Clare –'

Sarah had a ' 'Bye!' tossed her way, as her daughter left the kitchen.

'Clare! Will you be late?' she called to the closing door.

'Yes,' came a departing cry from the hall.

The coffee was ready. Sarah poured herself a cup and sat down at the kitchen table. The bacon rashers stared up slimily at her. Yugh. Clare was right; the thought of food at that time in the morning was obscene.

The bacon went back into the fridge. Sarah returned to her seat and took a sip of coffee.

What Clare had said had disturbed her, but it was only a mild disturbance. For a start, it probably meant nothing. 'It'll all be simpler when I move out' was the sort of line Clare frequently flung out as a warning shot in the armed truce which was their relationship.

And, if Clare did mean it, the possibility was not a completely new idea to Sarah. She knew that, even allowing for her daughter's alternating frosts and flare-ups, she had been lucky to have Clare around for the last two years. And she knew it was a situation that could not continue for ever. Part of the reason they got on each other's nerves so much was that they lived in such close proximity.

So it had to end some time. Sarah tried to curb the selfish maternal desire that that time should be as far away as possible. Because, apart from anything else, the corollary of Clare's departure would be that Sarah was left with just her mother.

She took a long, grateful swallow of coffee and tried to put the thought from her mind. She looked round the kitchen, refitted and decorated when they moved, but now showing the first hints of incipient shabbiness. The wallpaper over the cooker was slightly discoloured. The door on one of the units had slipped marginally out of alignment, so that it had to be lifted in closing to be secure on its magnetic catch. The paintwork at the bottom of the door to the hall was a little chipped, too often kicked shut when Sarah returned laden with shopping.

And by the back door there were two small chasms in the wall, where a shelf, fixed by Henry with inadequate Rawlplugging, had detached itself the first time any weight was put on it. Little incompetences like that were much more poignant reminders of her husband than other, grander symbols. And, in a way that she knew was perverse and ridiculous, Sarah felt that to block in those holes and decorate over them would be a tiny act of betrayal.

But she was not in a maudlin mood. And she was alone. Again she sipped luxuriously at her coffee. In many ways this was the best moment of the day. Alone, still, before the routine demands of living started.

The peace couldn't last. There was a creak on the stairs, then a soft padding of footsteps across the hall carpet, and almost before she heard the little finger-tap on her kitchen door, Sarah said, with resignation, 'Come in, Mother.'

*

Eleanor Prescott stood in the doorway, dressed and made up for the day. She was not of the generation that believed in 'slopping around in dressing-gowns'.

She smiled graciously. 'Good morning, Sarah darling.' She hesitated, as if uncertain. 'I wonder if I could . . .?'

Sarah, who knew that uncertainty was not a part of her mother's emotional vocabulary, drily continued the question for her, '. . . borrow some . . .?'

'Yes,' said Eleanor, and closed the door, satisfied.

But Sarah was determined to play the ritual out. 'Some what?'

'Er . . . how about milk?' suggested Eleanor.

'How about it? Yes, I'm sure you can borrow some.' Sarah rose and crossed to the fridge. 'Though how you managed to get through two pints overnight, I can't imagine.'

'Two pints? Really?'

'Saw them yesterday evening.' Sarah stood with her hand on the fridge door and looked back ironically at her mother.

'Where?'

'In your fridge, Mother. On the milk shelf. But I suppose you didn't think to look *there*.'

'No, I didn't, actually.'

The excuse was so blatant that Sarah couldn't help grinning. 'You know, Mother, the idea of that flat upstairs was that it was self-contained.'

'I know,' said Eleanor, with an answering grin. 'Well, it is, but I'm not.'

'So I've gathered.' Sarah relented. 'Do you want some coffee?'

But her mother hadn't completed her part of the ritual. 'I just came to borrow the milk.'

'Well, borrow some coffee, too. And a mug. And don't bother to take them away.'

Sarah turned to the coffee-machine, and heard her mother's

8

voice, asking, mock-tentative, from the doorway, 'May I borrow a chair, too?'

'Sit down!'

Eleanor Prescott installed herself cosily at the table and looked round with satisfaction. 'Have you had your breakfast then, Sarah?'

'Just coffee.'

'Oh, it's not enough for you. You should −'

It only took a look from Sarah to dry up the rest of that particular sentence. They sat opposite each other with their full cups of coffee and took the first swallow in silence. Sarah looked at her watch. Still another ten minutes before she'd have to start the daily tedium of washing and dressing. There were advantages in working near to home. Ten more minutes. Not quite alone, but at least, for the moment, in silence.

It couldn't last. Eleanor Prescott had the same abhorrence for silence that nature has for a vacuum. 'I heard you and Clare having your usual morning banter.'

'At least we're talking. She's actually quite perky at the moment. Not going through one of her phases of total non-communication.'

'Confides in you, does she?' asked Eleanor innocently.

'To an extent.'

'What − tells you everything?'

Sarah grinned ruefully. 'Not to that extent, no.'

'No,' said Eleanor. And in that monosyllable, her tone had changed. Its innocence had given way to a kind of slyness, of which Sarah's long experience made her instantly aware.

'What do you mean? You know something?'

'One hears rumours,' said her mother demurely.

'What?'

'Don't know if it's true.'

But Sarah had known her mother too long to be taken in by this show of diffidence. 'Mother, come on. What is it?'

It was never Eleanor Prescott's habit to give a direct answer to a question if she could avoid it. Once she was sure of her audience's attention, she preferred to go the pretty way. So, as if embarking on a completely new topic, she said, 'Clare's been getting home late a lot recently.'

'Yes, but —'

'I mean, she finishes at the building society at half-past five and she's never here before eight. Or if she is earlier, she rushes out again and —'

'Mother, if she —'

But Eleanor was not to be deflected from her story, or from her chosen manner of telling it. 'Not that much to do in this town, I'd have thought. Have you asked her what she does?'

'No,' Sarah replied firmly. 'I don't think parents should pry.'

If this remark had any relevance to herself, Eleanor chose to ignore it. 'Oh, no. Nor do I.' She paused. 'But when it's your own child, that's different.' She smiled innocently at her daughter. 'You mean you do know what she does, then?'

'Well, I know she sometimes plays badminton with friends, and she, well, she has a drink with friends or . . .' Sarah was annoyed to find herself getting increasingly flustered. 'I mean, she is eighteen, Mother. She's adult . . . by law, anyway. It's not my place to follow her every . . . I mean, it's up to her . . . I don't care, it's . . .' There was a long silence before Sarah finally had to surrender to her curiosity. 'What has she been doing?'

Eleanor rewarded herself with a small smile for having achieved the direct question she had been fishing for. But, once again, her reply was oblique. 'Well, Mrs Johnson from the Day Centre's grandson Terry works behind the bar at the Red Lion . . .'

Sarah said nothing, knowing by bitter experience that

Eleanor would make her revelations at her own pace and that any attempts to hurry her would only have the reverse effect.

'. . . and Terry's seen Clare in there more than once in the evenings.'

If that was all, Sarah had her response ready. 'So? She's old enough to drink legally. She often goes out with Gary and the rest of her crowd after work. Clare's very sensible about alcohol and I don't see why you should make a fuss about her going out for a drink with friends if —'

'Not friends,' said Eleanor, poising her bombshell neatly over its target. 'Friend.'

'What do you mean?'

'An Older Man.'

Sarah tried to escape the implications by flippancy. 'The same Older Man each time or is she working her way through the bowls club?'

'The same one each time.'

'Ah.'

Glowing from the reaction to her initial revelation, Eleanor proceeded to pile on the evidence. 'And Sylvia Waits from the Meals on Wheels has seen them together in the White Horse.'

'Oh.'

'Twice.'

'I wonder who he is . . .' mused Sarah, setting things up all too easily for her mother.

'I know,' Eleanor announced smugly.

Of course. She'd never have started the elaborate lead-up if she didn't. Sarah gave in. 'All right. Who?'

'Margaret Walton's cousin Pauline heard about him from Valerie Brown on the pension counter's sister Mary.'

'Good God,' Sarah murmured. 'The geriatric grapevine's been working overtime.' It was a source of minor, but continuing, irritation to her that her mother, thrown suddenly in her seventies into a town where she knew no one, had within weeks built up a network of acquaintance far more complex and numerous than Sarah's own.

Eleanor did not respond to her daughter's remark; she was too eager to continue her revelation. 'He does coaching at the tennis club,' she announced triumphantly.

Sarah tried flippancy again. 'The Older Man. He must be fit for his age.'

'Sarah, this is serious. This is Clare we're talking about.'

'I know. How old exactly is this man?'

'Well, Valerie Brown on the pension counter's sister Mary's gentleman friend Maurice is a groundsman at the tennis club and he reckons the Older Man's at least thirty-five.'

'Hmm,' said Sarah wistfully. 'That sounds quite young to me.'

'But not for Clare.'

'No, I suppose not.'

Sarah wanted to be alone. She wanted to work out her own reactions to the news without promptings from her mother. But then all her life she had wanted to work out her own reactions to things without promptings from her mother.

And the next prompt came sharply on its cue. 'Well, what are you going to do about it, Sarah?'

She hadn't got the answer to that one ready yet, but she fudged something together. 'I don't know. It is her life, after all. I'm not going to interfere. Clare can see who she likes so far as I'm concerned. It's up to her and . . .' She was silent as a new doubt crept into her mind. 'I wonder why she hasn't told me anything about it . . .'

This was an incautiously open invitation to Eleanor, whose memory was a comprehensive card-index of precedents from Sarah's own childhood, which could instantly be summoned up, given only a hint of a cue. She immediately had one ready for this occasion.

'*You* never told me when you went to see *Jailhouse Rock* with that teddy boy, Mick.'

'Oh, Mother . . .' Sarah growled wearily. 'How many times do I have to tell you – Mick wasn't a teddy boy. He'd just borrowed his father's jacket and it was too big for him.'

'But you never told me,' Eleanor persisted.

'No. Right, I didn't tell you. And you know why I didn't tell you? Because . . . quite frankly, Mother . . . I knew, if I did, I'd never hear the end of it. I knew you'd just witter on about it till –'

'And you think Clare feels any differently about you?'

Yes, she did think so. Or she hoped so. But, even as she thought it, the awful doubt that Clare might feel exactly about her as she did about her mother sidled into Sarah's mind, draining its small, carefully husbanded store of self-confidence.

She tried to bluster her way out. 'Mother, even you must admit that you've always been a nosy old bat.'

Eleanor did not rise to the insult. Instead, she smiled serenely and said, 'Sarah, to their daughters all mothers are nosy old bats – it's just something that goes with the job.'

As Sarah went through the automatic processes of washing and dressing, she felt slightly troubled by the two pieces of information she had received that morning.

The fact that Clare wanted to get away from the house and set up in a flat of her own was perhaps saddening. But not unpredictable. Nothing to worry about.

And the fact that she was seeing an Older Man in secret was wounding to her mother's self-image as her daughter's confidant. But, again, it was fairly natural behaviour in an eighteen-year-old. Again, nothing really to worry about.

But if the two facts were related – if Clare was planning to move into a flat *with* her Older Man – then they did become rather worrying.

Chapter 2

A 'Serious Talk'

Bygone Books was one of those shops which would raise the same question with anyone who bothered to think about it: How on earth does somewhere like that make money?

Its narrow, bow-windowed frontage was welcoming, but did not suggest a flourishing business. The few volumes displayed on a bookcase in the window were not the kind to be snapped up by professional bibliophiles, later to change hands for large sums at Christie's. It was always an intriguing selection, but one whose value had to be rated in terms of interest rather than money.

That morning, as Sarah entered the shop door, had she looked in the window (and she didn't, because she knew what was there), she would have seen a copy of Isaac D'Israeli's *Literary Character of Men of Genius*, John Timbs's *English Eccentrics and Eccentricities*, Samuel Butler's *Erewhon*, Erasmus Darwin's *The Botanic Garden* (opened to reveal a steel engraving of a Blake illustration), and an elderly edition of *Brewer's Dictionary of Phrase and Fable*. Mixed promiscuously in with these were more modern books, Patricia Highsmith's *Edith's Diary*, *The Compleet Molesworth* (open at a typically grotesque Ronald Searle drawing of a schoolmaster), and J. R. Ackerley's diaries, *My Sister and Myself*.

The selection seemed so random that it had clearly been assembled with considerable care, exactly reflecting the literary tastes of one person.

The interior of the shop which Sarah entered demonstrated the same quirky individuality. It was walled with shelves, many deep enough to take two layers of books. These were loaded to capacity, and every other surface had its little deposit of piled-up literature. There were cardboard boxes, also full of books, on the floor. The first impression was one of chaos.

And yet there was an order to it. Again the randomness suggested the existence of a controlling mind which knew to which pile every book in the shop belonged. There was even a visible, if eccentric, cataloguing system. Shelves were marked with narrow stickers on which an italic hand had written in brown ink such categories as 'Serious History', 'Light History', 'Fictional History', 'Funny Books that Make you Laugh', 'Humorous Books that Make you Smile', 'Good Old-Fashioned Detective Stories in which No One Really Gets Hurt' and 'Thrillers with Swastikas on the Front'.

It was obvious that the man who looked up mildly from his desk to greet Sarah over the top of his half-glasses was the owner of the personality which permeated the shop as strongly as the musty smell of damp-mottled paper.

Russell Bryant was in his early fifties. There was nothing in his manner to hint at his homosexuality and, indeed, but for his openness in talking about it, no one would have suspected that for eight years he had been quietly and happily married to a young man called Bob.

His smile of welcome to Sarah was completely genuine. She frequently suspected that he had 'taken on staff' not so much because of the volume of work he had to cope with, but simply because he got lonely in the shop all day by himself. (It was not the sort of set-up into which customers made much intrusion.) But she didn't question the reasons for her good fortune. The arrangement suited both of them very well, and that was what mattered.

She hung up her coat and scarf, and rubbed her hands together. 'Right, what do you want me to do?'

'Catalogues, I'm afraid.' Russell indicated two piles on his desk, one of photocopied sheets, the other of manila envelopes. 'I want to get all of these out today.'

Sarah drew up a chair and started to staple the sheets together, fold them up and insert them in their envelopes. It was one of those pleasantly mindless tasks which she got through by playing Time and Motion games. First, she experimented with a three-process system: stapling a pile, then folding them all, then inserting them all. When she got bored with that, she tried following through each one individually: stapling one catalogue, folding it, inserting it, and then moving on to the next.

Given the limited space on the book-laden desk, neither method was much more efficient than the other, but alternating the two passed the time amiably enough.

And the catalogues, incidentally, answered the universal question about Bygone Books. The shop made very little profit from its trickle of customers, most of whom left without making any purchases. It was from the mail-order side of the business that Russell made his money, and he was in daily correspondence with collectors and fellow dealers all over the world.

He worked companionably through the morning mail, while Sarah tried, without marked success, to increase her efficiency as an envelope-stuffer.

Russell piled up his correspondence, neatly tore up the envelopes and discarded the debris into a wicker wastepaper basket. He reached down to the floor to switch on the electric kettle. Then he folded his hands on his lap and looked at Sarah. 'You want to talk,' he said. 'Uncle Russell can tell.'

Sarah grinned. 'Yes. But I shouldn't.'

'Why ever not?'

'I'm here to work, not to talk.'

'Sarah, if I thought you had a brain whose every cell would be occupied by the task of putting catalogues in envelopes, then I might want you to keep silent. As it happens, I am confident of your ability to perform both actions without either suffering. And, incidentally, had you had the size of brain I described, I wouldn't have employed you.'

'Thank you. I think, picking through the verbiage of that, it could have been a compliment.'

'Think you're right.' Russell reached into a glass-fronted cupboard marked 'Supposedly Humorous Novels about International Academic Conferences' for a jar of Nescafé. 'And, in fact, your conversation *is* one of the reasons why I employed you.'

'But conversation should be a two-way process. All that happens with us is that I talk and you listen.'

'Temporary state of affairs.' Russell reached two mugs off the 'Big Mindless Books for Beaches' shelf. 'Roles could be reversed overnight and then you'd have to listen to me maundering on.'

'Oh dear,' said Sarah. 'Do I maunder?'

'No.'

'Meaning yes?'

'Well . . . Sometimes.'

'Hmm.' Sarah looked rueful. 'I can't see our roles reversing in a hurry.'

'Don't you believe it. Bob might suddenly walk out on me for a younger man.'

'No chance. You're one of the cosiest little couples I know.'

Russell shrugged. 'Other things happen. You and Henry seemed quite a cosy little couple . . .'

'Yes,' she agreed quietly, but without self-pity. 'Do you know, Russell, I think the thing I'm most grateful to you for is the fact that you talk about Henry's death. It's incredible – he died nearly two years ago and yet there are still people I see regularly who pretend that nothing's happened. It makes me feel as if I'm walking round with some terribly disfiguring birthmark that everyone's too sensitive to mention.'

Russell chuckled. 'Yes, I got that a bit when I "came out". To his dying day, my father just refused to believe it. Kept asking me if I'd got any girlfriends. "No, Dad," I'd reply every time, "I've got a boyfriend." "Don't be silly, Russell," he'd say. "I know about these things. You mean girlfriend."'

The kettle was boiling. Russell took a carton of milk off the tiny shelf marked 'Political Memoirs with a Sense of Humour', and made the coffee. He passed a cup across to Sarah and asked, 'Anyway, what's troubling you today . . . in particular? The absent husband, the all-too-present mother, or the errant daughter . . .?'

'It's Clare. She's having a clandestine affair.'

Russell rubbed his hands together with relish. 'Ooh, what

a very eighteenth-century phrase. And is this a full-blown affair with two veg and all the trimmings?'

'I don't know.' And Sarah told him what she did know. Which, in spite of Eleanor's exhaustive research work, wasn't really a great deal.

'Well,' said Russell when she'd finished, 'can't you ask Clare about it?'

'I suppose I'll have to. Have a "serious talk" with her. Come the heavy mother.' She grimaced with dissatisfaction at the phrase. 'Doesn't sound right, does it? Hasn't got quite the same idiomatic thrust as "come the heavy father".'

'Not quite, no.'

'Anyway, it probably won't do any good. Trying to have a "serious talk" with Clare is about as easy as catching an eel with a bit of string.' She sighed and stuffed another catalogue firmly into its envelope. 'Oh dear. This is just another of those hundred times a week when I want to ask Henry. Get his reaction.'

'Yes,' said Russell gently, 'it must be hard making the major decisions on your own.'

'It's not the major decisions. Usually it's something utterly mundane and practical. Does the right-hand mains switch control the old round-pin socket in the spare room? Just need a quick answer. It's things like that, you know, that could get me into spiritualism. Not deep emotional communication, just practical advice. "Hello, Henry. Should I change the antifreeze in the car? One knock for yes, two knocks for no. Does the standing order for the gas include the service agreement on the boiler?"'

'And should Clare be moving into a flat with this Older Man?' asked Russell, pulling down the balloon of her fantasy.

'Yes.' She looked pensive. 'Fathers are supposed to take it very hard when their daughters start going out with boys.

Henry died before Clare was into all that in a big way. I wonder what he would have said. So many ways I wonder how he would have developed . . .'

'I'm sorry . . .' said Russell, perhaps anticipating tears.

But the emotional outburst he got was of anger rather than sorrow. 'No, I am not being maudlin for once. Just frustrated! I'd like to know, and I'm never going to know!' She quietened down. 'I am worried about Clare, though. She hasn't really had any serious boyfriends. Most of the time she goes around in a group with her punk friend Gary and a load of others. I'm afraid she's still very emotionally vulnerable. She could easily get mixed up with someone totally unsuitable. I mean, Henry's death hit her terribly hard.'

'Presumably why she's going for an Older Man.'

'Yes, I suppose so.' Sarah looked down guiltily at her empty hands. In her burst of anger, the stapling, folding and inserting had got suspended. 'I'm sorry. You know, there are machines that'd put these catalogues in envelopes quicker than I'm doing them.'

'Ah yes,' Russell agreed, 'but no machine would have your special feature.'

'What's that?'

He spread his hands wide, as if stating the obvious. 'The built-in-soap-opera function. Daily accounts of your mother and daughter's doings.'

She was suitably chastened. 'I'm sorry. I know I do witter on.'

'Sarah, believe me, I don't mind.'

'Thank you,' she said, gratified.

Russell smiled almost imperceptibly, as he murmured, 'No, I always like background noise when I'm working.'

'Thank you,' said Sarah, less gratified, cramming an unoffending catalogue savagely into its envelope.

*

It was half-past seven. Sarah was in her sitting-room, thinking that she really did fancy a drink. But some outdated Calvinist instinct always made her feel slightly guilty about drinking on her own. And the same Calvinism also suggested strongly that, if she was going to have a drink, she should really ask her mother down to join her. And she hadn't yet got the strength to do that. Not until she'd had a drink, anyway.

The sound of the front door opening put the drink problem from her mind. It must be Clare. No way round it – the 'serious talk' was going to have to happen. Sarah leapt to her feet. You had to be quick to catch Clare these days.

Her daughter was in the kitchen with her back to the door as Sarah entered. 'Ah. Clare.'

'Hello, Mummy,' said Clare, without turning round.

'I thought I heard you come in.'

'Yes, I just did. Got to go and have a bath,' Clare said brusquely, hoping to cut off the conversation before it started.

'Mm. Actually, Clare, I wanted a chat. Maybe over supper we could just –'

'Don't want supper. I'm having this.' She turned to reveal that each of her hands held a chocolate digestive biscuit spread with golden syrup.

'Oh, Clare,' Sarah grimaced. 'That is quite revolting. And, anyway, it's not enough to –'

'Don't start that again. You said it all at breakfast.' Clare crammed one of the biscuits into her mouth and swept past her mother into the hall. 'Sorry, I must get on,' she mumbled through the crumbs.

Sarah followed after her. 'Clare. Clare, I wanted to talk.'

Clare froze dramatically with one hand on the banister and said in a voice heavy with foreboding, 'Oh, God.'

Having snatched a minute of her daughter's attention, Sarah

wasn't going to waste it. 'You were late back again this evening.'

'Quick, aren't you? Give you a watch and you can tell the time.'

Sarah recognized the technique, because it was one she frequently used with her own mother. Direct rudeness could lead to a row, and in that row an undesirable subject could get lost. She was determined not to fall into the trap.

'Clare', she said evenly, 'I don't want you to make me angry.'

'I'm not *trying* to make you angry. It just seems to happen whenever we talk. So the logical conclusion is that we don't talk. Seems straightforward enough to me.'

Again, Sarah resisted the reaction that Clare was trying to provoke. She maintained the evenness of her tone. 'Listen, I don't think you've been working late or playing badminton or –'

'I never said I had.' Clare shoved the other syrup-covered biscuit into her mouth and started determinedly up the stairs.

'I think you've been drinking in the Red Lion.'

'Ah.' Clare froze.

'Or the White Horse. With a man.'

Clare turned angrily to her mother. 'And I think you've been listening to malicious gossip.'

'No, I've been talking to your grandmother.'

'That's what I said.'

Sarah tried to take the edge off the situation. Moving on to the bottom stair, she said gently, 'Clare, please listen. I have been through the sort of thing you're feeling. I can help. I'm not being nosy; I just want you to tell me about this man you're seeing.'

'And that's *not* being nosy? I'd hate to see you when you *are* being nosy.'

As anticipated, the interview was not proving easy. Sarah kept a tight rein on her mounting anger and continued in her gentle tone, 'I am thinking of you, Clare. If he's nice, why are you being so secretive about him? It's the deceit that hurts. Why can't you tell me?'

Clare stared expressionlessly at her mother.

'Oh,' Sarah burst out in exasperation, 'I might just as well be talking to myself.'

'You are,' said Clare and marched up the stairs.

Sarah felt an idiot trailing along after her daughter, but, having got this far into the conversation, she wasn't going to let the subject go.

'I just want to know what sort of man he is. I hate to think of someone stringing you along.'

Clare walked firmly across the landing towards her bedroom. 'He is not stringing me along. He's serious.'

'Good.' Sarah hovered by the bedroom door. 'And this talk of moving into a flat . . . do you mean moving in with him?'

Clare, who had just picked her towelling bath-robe off a chair, turned and demanded defiantly, 'Why not?'

'No reason,' said Sarah automatically. Then, after a pause, she continued, 'Well, some reasons.' She paused again. 'Quite a few reasons, actually, when I come to think of it. I mean, I know he's older than you. The age difference might be a bit worrying. He might be married or . . .' She saw the contempt in Clare's eyes, and hated the scene she was having to play. 'I really am thinking of you, love. I don't want you to get hurt. I have felt what you're feeling, Clare.'

For a moment her daughter seemed to soften. 'Have you?'

Sarah smiled. 'You're very like me in many ways.'

'Mummy, please don't say that.'

'Why ever not?'

Clare slung her bath-robe over her arm and strode across to the bathroom door before replying. When she did, it was in a voice of icy fury.

'Mummy, I am only eighteen. I have acres and acres of life ahead of me. And to get through it I have to have some hope. If I really believed I was going to end up like you . . . well, it'd be like living under a death sentence!'

With a perfect sense of timing which, even through her anger, Sarah was forced to acknowledge, Clare slammed the bathroom door.

Her mother stood for a moment on the landing, fuming, but conquered the instinct to retaliate. She stumped back downstairs.

Now she really *did* need that drink.

She had had a couple before she remembered her good Calvinist intention to invite Eleanor down to join her. Suitably braced, she set off upstairs. On the landing she heard disgruntled sloshing noises and running water from the bathroom. In her present kind of mood Clare was quite capable of spending over an hour in the bath. It was her regular recourse at times of emotional crisis. An hour of wallowing, adding more and more hot water until she wrinkled up like a prune, could sometimes put her into a better mood. Sarah hoped it would on this occasion.

She went on up the next flight of stairs, at the top of which was a tiny landing and the door to Eleanor's flat. In Edwardian times when the house had been built, this floor had been attics and servants' rooms. Eleanor frequently alluded to this, constantly referring to her flat as 'my little servant's quarters'. She also frequently complained about the state of their décor, and how her 'little kitchen-diner' in particular could 'really do with brightening-up'.

When the attic space had been converted, although the

connecting door remained, an exterior staircase had been built, so that people living in the flat could come and go without passing through the main house. This was a fact of architecture which Sarah's mother seemed, with increasing frequency, to have forgotten.

Sarah heard through the door the raucous braying of a television situation-comedy audience. Eleanor, who suffered from intermittent diplomatic and tactical deafness, always had the television on very loud. Sarah tapped on the door with her knuckle.

Instantly, the television was switched off. Seconds later, Eleanor appeared at the door, graciously patting her hair into place.

'Good evening, Sarah dear.'

'Hello, Mother. I was just having a drink. Wondered if you fancied coming down for one . . .?'

'Oh, that is kind of you.'

'I mean, unless there's something you want to watch on the box . . .?'

'Oh, no, dear. There's so rarely anything worth seeing. I haven't switched the thing on for weeks.'

'Oh,' said Sarah. 'Haven't you?'

Downstairs, when Eleanor was equipped with a stiff gin and tonic and Sarah a third glass of red wine, the conversation was quickly steered towards Clare.

Sarah tried to steer it firmly away again, shrugging the subject off with 'You know what Clare's like. Absolutely hopeless trying to get anything out of her.'

But Eleanor wasn't going to be satisfied so easily. 'You did talk to her, did you?'

'Oh yes. At least I managed to find her for once. Usually, when I want to have "a serious talk" with her, she disappears.'

'Yes.' Eleanor nodded sagely. 'She goes down to the basement.'

'Does she? What on earth's the attraction of the basement?'

'You aren't there, dear,' Eleanor replied with a sweet smile.

'Thank you.' This was news, though. The basement was only used for storage. When they'd bought the house, Henry and Sarah had had grandiose schemes for converting it into games rooms and studies – he'd even talked of installing a sauna down there – but those ideas, like so many others, had died with him. And now getting the basement organized, in the same way as filling in the scars in the kitchen wall, would somehow seem disloyal to Henry.

Sarah knew she was stupid about things like that, knew that she would have to get the place organized at some point, but she kept putting it off. The question of the basement raised other ominous issues – particularly her recurrent internal debate about whether she should stay in the house or not. It was too big for the three of them, and when Clare did actually move out . . .

But she had no time to get back into that particular cycle of conjecture. Eleanor was, as ever, probing for more information. 'But, Sarah dear, didn't Clare tell you *anything*?'

'Not much.'

Eleanor looked pensive. 'Maybe *I* should have a little talk with her . . .'

'I don't think we're reduced to that, Mother.'

The mother in question bridled. 'Clare and I sometimes have a great rapport. Grandmothers and granddaughters frequently do. The sympathy sort of skips a generation.'

Sarah ignored the implied slight. 'Yes, I know all that. But I think this one is just between me and her.'

'Oh, very well.' Eleanor shrugged and took a sip at her drink. Then she granted her daughter a smile of infinite understanding. 'I do know what you're going through, you know.'

'Do you?'

'Oh yes. I have felt what you're feeling, Sarah.'

'Have you?' asked Sarah warily.

'You're very like me in many ways.'

Sarah winced. 'Mother. Please don't say that.'

Chapter 3

'Coming the Heavy Mother'

Sarah stood irresolute inside the door of Bygone Books and asked for the third time in half an hour, 'Are you sure you don't mind me going?'

Russell looked at her with undisguised amusement, but did not bother to answer this time.

'I just don't feel I should be leaving the shop,' she prevaricated.

'The catalogues have been sent out, the mail orders dealt with, there are no auctions today, and I think I can cope' – Russell gestured ironically to the empty space around him – 'with today's inundation of customers. Go on. You're just making excuses. You want to avoid this confrontation.'

'Yes,' she confessed.

'Off you go. It's what Henry would have done.'

She hoped that was true. It became increasingly difficult, with the passage of time and moral decisions that grew ever more complex, to project what Henry would have done. In some ways, he had been deeply conventional. Sarah had even teased him about it. In the balance of their relationship, he had been the moral fuddy-duddy, she the freethinker. But with Henry no longer in the picture to provide comparisons, Sarah was forced to face her own latent conservatism.

'Oh dear,' she sighed. 'I suppose there will come a day when I do something without wondering what Henry would have done.'

'I'm sure there will. But it hasn't come yet.' Russell made a shooing gesture with his hands. 'Go on, off to the O K Corral with you.'

Sarah nodded, and reached positively towards the door handle. But once again she vacillated. 'It's going to be awfully embarrassing when I get to the tennis club. How shall I start talking to him?'

'Say you're having trouble with your backhand.'

'Hmm.' Another procrastinating thought. 'How will I know who he is?'

'Ask for him. Do you know his name?'

She nodded. 'Nick. I got that from Valerie Brown on the pension counter's sister Mary's gentleman friend Maurice.'

'I should have guessed.'

Guilt now joined in the conspiracy to delay Sarah further. 'I do feel awful about Clare. Going behind her back. As if I was the wicked stepmother offering Snow White a poisoned apple.'

'Go *on*!' urged Russell in exasperation, and then dropped into song. 'With your shovel and your pick and your ar-sen-ic, hi-ho, hi-ho, hi . . .'

Another positive 'Yes' from Sarah. Then 'Are you *sure* you'll be all right?'

Russell waved an old book at her by way of reply. 'With a "first" of Henty's *Under Drake's Flag*, I will be in seventh heaven. Nothing I relish more than a cosy afternoon's swash-buckling.'

Sarah still wavered by the door.

'Oh, do go, Sarah! Just go! Up to the tennis club with you.'

'Yes. I won't be long . . . I'll be back as soon as . . . You know, it'll just be like a late lunch . . . I'll . . . um . . .'

'Sarah, I don't mind if you stay and play a couple of sets with him.'

'Right. O K.' For the umpteenth time Sarah checked her hair in a glass-fronted bookcase. 'Now . . . got my handbag, coat, umbrella . . . anything else I need?'

'Shotgun . . .?' Russell suggested mildly.

The tennis club looked a bit rundown. Partly it was seasonal. The would-be Boris Beckers and Steffi Grafs were back at school, leaving the courts to grey-haired tracksuited men staving off arthritis, and thick-thighed mothers vainly strug-gling to recover their figures after the last baby. They were all involved in games, long slow games of endless lobs; none of them was being coached. Feeling increasingly conspicuous by the minute, Sarah drifted towards the clubhouse.

It was a one-storey building, only a few steps up from a Nissen hut. The white paint on its walls had flaked and discoloured, the green metal frames of its windows were freckled with rust. Perhaps with the benefit of sunlight and a teeming crowd taking their drinks outside to watch the mixed doubles, it could have looked convivial. On a dull day in September it was the sort of place British prisoners-of-war would have tunnelled out of.

Sarah took a deep breath and pushed open the blistered

green door. Inside a few round tables and straight-backed wooden chairs clustered together for comfort on a floor with the faded markings of a badminton court. On the walls dull gold leaf on dusty boards recorded past tournament triumphs.

There were only two people in the room. Behind the bar an elderly man, engrossed in a copy of the *Sun*, barely looked up as she entered. And, on a stool with his back to her, a man in a tracksuit appeared to be eating something.

Her heels clacked, unnaturally loud, as she crossed to the bar. Her first 'Excuse me' came out with no volume at all, but the second dragged the barman's attention away from Page Three.

'Good afternoon. What can I do for you?'

Sarah cleared her throat. 'Erm. Yes. Thank you. I was, er, looking for the coach. Someone called Nick.'

The barman nodded towards the other man, who diverted his attention from his toasted cheese sandwich and gave Sarah far too charming a smile.

'That's me,' he said. 'I'm Nick. Can I get you a drink?'

There was no doubt about it, he was attractive. Sarah looked at him covertly as he joked with the barman and ordered their second drinks. Oh yes, she could understand how Clare could be swept off her feet by someone like that. Particularly someone who, for an eighteen-year-old, carried the additional cachet of being an Older Man.

He placed another white wine in front of her.

'Thank you.'

He raised his glass of Budweiser. 'Cheers.'

She echoed the toast and took a grateful sip. She was, feeling marginally more relaxed. At least the subject had been broached. And so far he hadn't either hit her or laughed in her face.

She grimaced apologetically. 'I'm sorry. I do feel rather awful about this.'

'Oh, you shouldn't,' he said with another of those smiles. 'I think it's rather magnificent. Very brave of you to come and beard your daughter's seducer in his den.'

Sarah started a little giggle, which drained away suddenly as she echoed, 'Seducer?'

'I use the term figuratively.'

'Do you?' asked Sarah, a little uncertain.

Nick gave a charming, but uninformative laugh, so she pressed on, 'I'm sorry. I feel awful being here. It's just, you know, I feel responsible for Clare and she was being so secretive about you and . . .'

'Have you vetted all her boyfriends?'

'Vetted?' she asked in alarm.

He grinned. 'It's an expression.'

'Oh, yes. Yes, of course. Sorry. Well, the answer to your question is no. Clare hasn't had that many boyfriends.' Sarah tried to think if there had been any who really justified the title. Gary, the pink-haired punk, was the boy whom Clare saw most often, but Sarah thought the relationship was probably platonic (a view not, incidentally, shared by Eleanor). However, it wouldn't do to diminish her daughter's image by admitting her total inexperience. 'Anyway, most of her boyfriends she's actually brought home, and they've only been friends from school and . . . You are a lot older than she is.'

He shrugged. 'Ten years, maybe. I'm thirty-four.'

'Clare is eighteen.'

That did throw him. It took a second or two before he responded. 'Only eighteen. She's mature for her age.'

This idea had never struck Sarah before. Much of the time it seemed to her that Clare was irredeemably infantile. But maybe to an outsider things looked different.

'She's very attractive, too,' Nick continued. 'Looks

33

remarkably like you. I expect you often get mistaken for sisters.'

It was the oldest line in the book, and Sarah felt ridiculous for blushing at it. But since Henry's death, she had been starved of praise, and it was warming to hear a compliment again – even one as corny as that.

'So she's only eighteen . . .' Nick mused.

Sarah put the compliment from her mind. If she was ever going to get round to 'coming the heavy mother', now was the moment.

'I mean, obviously,' she began with confidence, 'I don't have any hang-ups about . . .' a little gulp rather let her down, 'sex outside marriage.'

'Of course not,' Nick agreed gravely.

'I don't think many people do nowadays.' She emitted a little nervous laugh.

'No.'

'But when my daughter starts talking about moving in with someone, I feel I should at least *meet* the person concerned.'

Again Nick was thrown. 'Moving in with?'

'What? Hadn't you discussed it?'

'Well . . .' He looked pensive. 'I suppose things have been said that might be interpreted in a way that . . . Hmm.' He looked with unsettling directness into Sarah's eyes. 'Are you asking me to stop seeing her?'

This was presumably the point that she had been hoping to reach. The whole purpose of the confrontation had been to discuss this question. But now the moment had arrived, Sarah felt totally confused and flustered. 'No, no, of course not. It's not my place to . . . Oh God, I feel awful. I shouldn't be here.' Rather than being a forceful 'heavy mother', she found to her horror that she was starting to confess her weakness. 'You see, I'd got all worked up about how terribly unsuitable you were going to be, and now I meet you, and you're so normal, and nice, and I can understand exactly what she sees in you and . . .'

Nick maintained his disconcerting stare. There was also the tiniest twitch of a smile on his lips as he asked, 'Can you?'

Sarah floundered deeper into the mire. 'Well, I mean, I can see what an eighteen-year-old would see in someone who . . . um . . . well, it's . . . you know . . .'

He let a long silence rub in her confusion, then, with a hint of mischief in his eye, he nodded. 'Yes. I didn't realize Clare was quite so serious about it . . .' He appeared to reach a decision. 'Perhaps I *should* stop seeing her. Would it make you feel better if I did?'

Now she had really achieved what 'coming the heavy mother' had been aiming at, but the triumph didn't lessen her discomposure. 'Um . . . Well . . . No, I don't want to break up something that she's . . .'

This time Nick helped her out. In a very positive and responsible voice, he announced, 'I think it might be better all round if I stopped seeing her.'

The sense of relief was enormous. Sarah couldn't work out all the ramifications of it instantly, but at least a decision had been taken. And, even better, she hadn't been the one who had to take it.

She smiled at him gratefully, but Nick's next words again destroyed her fragile equilibrium.

With an unmistakable glint of devilment he said, 'No, I think I should stop seeing Clare . . . and start seeing you instead.'

'Oh dear,' said Sarah.

When she got back to Bygone Books, she felt better. Partly, it was having three glasses of wine inside her (Nick had insisted on 'one for the road'); but also she felt she'd got things sorted out a bit. Oh, he'd kept on with that silly line about going out with her, but she could recognize it for what it was — just a joke. And it had, she had to confess, been mildly flattering.

But, no, she really thought she'd sorted out things a bit for Clare. She hadn't deliberately broken up the relationship; it was just that, when Nick realized how seriously Clare was taking it, he had retreated very quickly.

In other words, the confrontation had been successful. The 'heavy mother' had maybe, in the event, proved somewhat lightweight, but she had achieved her goal.

Russell looked up mildly from his Henty novel, but passed no comment on the fact that it was a quarter to four. He did, however, want a full blow-by-blow account of what had happened. And Sarah, tactically editing out a few of the blows which she didn't think were really relevant, gave it to him.

At the end of her narrative, he nodded in admiration. 'So Nick packed his tents, quitted the field, and left you triumphant?'

But somehow, in the telling of it, Sarah's sense of triumph had trickled away, to be replaced by an unaccountable flatness. 'Yes, I suppose he did, really.'

'Congratulations. Your maternal duty achieved. Henry would be proud of you.'

By now the void left by the retreat of triumphant feelings was quickly filling with guilt. 'The trouble is, it's gone too far. I didn't actually want to break up the affair. I don't want to hurt Clare.'

'But, come on, you must be relieved.'

Sarah supposed relief was one of the ingredients in the new confusion of her thoughts. She tried to rationalize them. 'I don't know. I don't think the affair would have lasted, so perhaps it's better that it finishes sooner rather than later. I mean, I'm sure he wasn't as serious about her as she was about him. He certainly backed off very quickly when I mentioned her idea about their moving in together. No,' she concluded in a businesslike manner, 'I think he's just one of those, you know, attractive, amusing, lively sort of men who've got a lot of charm. Good-looking. Good company.'

'Sounds fun,' said Russell, in one of those rare moments which reminded Sarah of his sexual orientation.

'Oh yes,' she went on dismissively, trying to convince herself. 'But obviously Nick's the sort who's going to chat up anything in a skirt. Not very stable.' She made light of the admission. 'I mean he was almost chatting me up.'

Russell shook his head gravely. 'A sure sign of instability.'

'Thank you very much.' She grinned, but she wasn't really at ease. 'I still feel rather awful, from Clare's point of view. But I'm sure it is what Henry would have done. If he'd still been alive, the same confrontation would have taken place.'

'Except,' said Russell innocently, 'presumably he wouldn't have been chatted up . . .?'

'No, presumably not.' Sarah moved firmly towards a box of books that needed sorting. 'Anyway, it's done,' she pronounced with finality. 'I just hope it doesn't hit Clare's confidence too badly. I mean, obviously, there are thousands more men about, more suitable men, but it's hard to realize that when you're eighteen. I wonder if –'

Her conjectures were cut short by the telephone ringing. Russell answered it, and then, with a sardonic smile, held the receiver towards her.

'Who?' Sarah mouthed.

But he wasn't going to help her. He just maintained his infuriating smile, and with a grimace of annoyance, she took the receiver.

'Hello?'

'Sarah. Nick.'

'Ah. Hello.'

Russell grinned at her discomfiture.

Nick's voice continued, lazy and intimate in her ear. 'I was wondering about meeting for that drink we talked about.'

'You may have talked about meeting for a drink. I didn't.'

'Oh, come on,' he shrugged verbally, 'don't let's get side-tracked by pronouns. How about the Red Lion at six?'

'No,' she replied righteously. 'I can't. I don't think it's a good idea.'

It was the right answer, she knew. The proper answer. But it did make her feel slightly wistful.

Anyway, Nick wasn't going to be shaken off quite so easily. 'Pity,' he said. 'I wanted to talk about Clare.'

He knew she'd respond to that, and she did.

'I've been thinking,' he continued, 'about what you were saying.'

'Oh?'

'Think we should just have a little further chat. You know, neither of us wants Clare to be hurt, do we?' he asked with suspect earnestness.

'No . . .' she replied hesitantly, aware of his emotional blackmail and yet half-welcoming it.

'So what do you say?'

'Well. All right. A quick drink.'

'Good.' He sounded annoyingly self-satisfied.

'But not the Red Lion,' she said hastily.

'Why not? What's wrong with it?'

'Well . . .' It was a bit difficult to explain.

'What?' Nick's voice insisted.

The answer came out all in a rush. 'Mrs Johnson from the Day Centre's grandson Terry works behind the bar.'

A mystified 'Oh' came from the other end of the line.

When an alternative rendezvous had been arranged and the phone-call concluded, Sarah made no comment.

Nor did Russell.

But was she being hypersensitive to detect a slight quizzical lift to one of his eyebrows?

Chapter 4

Nothing in it

There was nothing in it. Sarah knew there was nothing in it. Just pleasant to have someone else in her life for a change.

And how far Nick was into her life was a question she didn't like to investigate too deeply. Her memory and her whole emotional system were still so full of Henry that there was not yet a possibility of anyone taking over in that way. Sometimes she resented the hold her dead husband still had on her. He was no longer there to give anything in the relationship – why the hell couldn't he just let go of her, leave her alone, give her at least the chance of meeting someone else?

These thoughts would always be followed by guilt at their

vehemence, guilt that she even dared think them, and then, as the passion slowly subsided, it would be replaced by a wistfulness, a nostalgic appreciation of what Henry had been, of what he had given her while he was alive.

But the fact remained that, whether she liked it or not, he still dominated her life. Henry was the dog that still lay selfishly across the manger of her emotions. There was not yet room for anyone else. With feelings that varied from fury to wry acceptance, she knew that, even if the rightest of Mr Rights walked into her life, she would not yet be able to allow him to stay there.

Which was why Nick was such good news. He did not appear to want to share her life. He liked seeing her every now and then. He was charming to her when they did meet. He complimented her. He amused her.

There was also a slight tingling of naughtiness about the proceedings. For obvious reasons, they wanted to keep Clare ignorant of their meetings, and Sarah didn't want Eleanor to know about them either. This was for the same reason that she'd never wanted Eleanor to know anything about any of her relationships with men – namely, that once her mother had elicited the smallest detail about any new male friend, Sarah would never hear the end of it.

Fortunately, Nick seemed quite happy to respect her desire for secrecy.

Her other anxiety, that Clare was going to be terribly cast down by the break-up with Nick, did not materialize. In fact, her daughter seemed to remain remarkably cheerful. Not that they saw much of each other. Now that Sarah had the beginnings of a social life of her own, and Clare seemed to be going out as much as ever, their meetings were reduced to snatches of conversation in the mornings and occasional passings on the stairs.

So, basically, Sarah and Nick had a good time. And Sarah

enjoyed herself in an unpressured way that she hadn't experienced for ages.

Of course, there were pressures. Sex, as usual, loomed ominously. So far that had been restricted to the odd kiss and cuddle in the car, but Nick left her in no doubt that he'd like it to go further. So far his pressure had been gentle, but he was getting more insistent. Sarah recognized that that pressure might end the relationship. Since Henry's death she had suffered deep pangs of sexual loneliness and deprivation, but at the same time a kind of numbness. She wasn't yet ready for another full sexual relationship – or if she was, it would have to be with someone she loved more than she did Nick.

But that was part of his attraction for her, the knowledge that the relationship couldn't last, that it was never going to go the distance. Because its duration was finite, she could relax and enjoy it.

And also, she did find that, the more time she spent with Nick, the more she liked him. Maybe he was starting a slow thaw in her frozen emotions.

It was a couple of weeks after their first meeting at the tennis club. They had had a few drinks at a pub in a village called Stipton, discreetly distant from the prying eyes of the town. In the car, during their farewells, Nick's hands had strayed a little more adventurously than hitherto, and Sarah had found, with some surprise, that, whatever her mind was doing, her body was not completely uninterested.

She had said the right things, however, and they had parted chastely and on good terms. There was something exciting about it all, though, stealing kisses in parked cars, a kind of teenage frisson. For the first time since Henry's death, forty-two-year-old Sarah felt nearer to her thirties than her fifties.

So she was childishly cheerful as she let herself into the

house. And relaxed. She felt as if she would sleep deeply that night. No need to have an alcoholic nightcap or the guilty self-questioning over whether or not she should take a sleeping pill.

She switched off the hall light and was about to go upstairs when she noticed a gleam from under the kitchen door. Oh, damn, she must have left it switched on when she hurried out after work.

She opened the door, and was confronted by Eleanor, in her dressing-gown, sitting at the kitchen table over a cup of Ovaltine.

'Ah. Mother. I thought you'd be in bed. Or at least up in your own flat,' she added pointedly.

Eleanor accorded her the munificence of a smile. 'Well, I thought, dear, that, when you did . . . eventually . . . get back, you'd want to pop up to the flat to say goodnight, and if I were down here, it'd save you the trouble of the stairs.'

'That was very thoughtful of you,' said Sarah, tight-lipped. Then, loudly, 'Goodnight, Mother.' There was a silence. 'There, I've said it.'

Eleanor either was, or could appear to be, impervious to irony. 'Nice evening, dear?' she asked with a guileless smile.

'Yes, thank you.'

'Go anywhere nice?'

This inquiry got another frosty 'Yes, thank you.'

'Good.' Eleanor, immaculately timing her own scene, took a long sip of Ovaltine, before embarking on a characteristic *non sequitur*. 'You know Mrs Graham the receptionist at the surgery's brother-in-law's stepson Colin?'

'No. No, I don't believe I do,' Sarah replied, moving to the sink to wash up Eleanor's milk saucepan.

'Well, he works as a barman at the Spotted Cow at Stipton.'

The saucepan froze in mid-air. 'Oh. Does he?'

'I mean, I'm the last one to interfere . . .' Eleanor lied.

'Of course. But.'

'*But* I do think you should be a bit careful. I mean, what you do with your life, who you see, that's your own concern. I'd be the last one to pry . . .'

'The very last,' Sarah murmured with resignation, and then again, 'But.'

'*But* I wonder why you're being so secretive. If he's nice, why don't you tell me? It's the deceit that hurts. But I don't like the idea of someone stringing you along. Then there's the age difference. Or he might be married for all you know or . . .'

As Eleanor got into her stride, Sarah closed her eyes. And wished she could close her ears as easily.

Russell watched with amusement as Sarah slammed books into the 'Classics that are Surprisingly Readable' shelf. 'Been talking to your mother by any chance . . .?' he hazarded.

'Yes,' she fumed. 'Oh, honestly! I really don't think I can stand it much longer. The way she witters on. I am forty-two, for God's sake.'

'"There are orphanages for children who have lost their parents – oh! why, why are there no harbours of refuge for grown men who have not yet lost them",' he quoted.

'Dead right. Who is it?'

'Samuel Butler. One of my favourites.'

'Well, he knew what he was talking about.' Sarah growled with frustration. 'Life at home is very difficult at the moment.'

'Clare's still OK?'

'Yes. Remarkably sunny, actually. On the rare occasions I see her.'

'Does she know?'

'Know what?'

44

'About you seeing Nick.'

Sarah coloured. 'Oh, I wouldn't put it as strongly as that.'

'You can't put it much weaker than "seeing", Sarah.'

'No, I suppose not. Well, I haven't told her. I'm starting to feel a bit guilty about it. No, I will have a chat with Clare soon.'

'I think you'd better,' said Russell.

Sarah nodded. But she didn't want to. She had an ominous feeling that telling her daughter the truth would somehow spell the end of her meetings with Nick. And, increasingly, she didn't want them to end.

But that was, relatively speaking, a minor problem. 'Anyway, things with Clare are fine. It's my bloody mother who's driving me mad.'

'So what else is new?'

'It's a matter of the degree to which I'm being driven mad.' She sighed wearily. 'Oh, I don't know. It's not having Henry there as a buffer. When he was around, I could cope with her.' She allowed herself a moment of self-pity. 'Lots of things I could do if Henry was still here.'

'And a few you couldn't . . .' said Russell casually.

'Like?'

'Clandestine drinks with John McEnroe.'

'Oh.' Sarah felt herself blushing again. 'There's nothing serious in that.'

'No . . .?'

'No,' said Sarah, hoping she meant it as firmly as she said it. 'Just company.' She smiled a little wistfully. 'He's fun, though. Very pleasant. It can't last, but it's nice to be treated like a woman for a change.'

Russell nodded sympathetically.

The more Sarah found herself liking Nick, the more important one question loomed in her life. It started as just a tiny doubt, when she had been talking to Clare about the mysterious Older Man, but after her own meeting with Nick, it had begun to swell. And now, fuelled by Eleanor's insinuations, it was full to bursting point. There was no way round it. She would have to ask him directly.

They were sitting one evening in another pub in another village (although Eleanor's geriatric grapevine knew about the relationship, it was still important to keep Clare in ignorance). For once, their conversation was a little sluggish, and Sarah decided that the doubt had to be removed before it would flow again.

'Nick . . .' she began casually.

'Hmm?'

'There's something I want to ask you.'

He gave her the benefit of his straight, unsettling stare. 'Yes?'

She looked down at her glass. 'I wanted to ask you when I was worried about you going round with Clare . . .'

'Fire ahead.'

'Yes.' Sarah twisted her glass round on its mat. Now she had got to the point, she felt embarrassed.

Nick grinned. 'You're making it sound awfully momentous. Real Spanish Inquisition stuff. What is it?'

'Well . . .'

'When did I last see my father?' Nick suggested.

'No.' His joking wasn't making it any easier.

'Then what?'

Sarah took a deep breath and raised her eyes to meet his. Then she asked the question. 'Are you married?'

He smiled his disarming smile. 'Oh, now, Sarah, surely you don't think it's proper for married men to run around with nubile teenagers? Or indeed with equally nubile widows.'

'I wouldn't have said we were running around.'

'You're giving me the runaround.'

'No, I'm not. I'm . . .' Sarah stopped herself. She wasn't going to fall for his diversionary tactics. 'This isn't answering my question.'

'About being married?'

'Yes.'

'Let's say you need have no worries on that score.'

But she wasn't going to let him off the hook so easily. 'That hasn't answered it, either.'

'No.' He took a long drink from his beer, and then looked straight into her eyes. 'So . . . you want a straight yes or no to the question: Am I married?'

'Yes.'

'No,' he said firmly.

'Ah,' said Sarah, with a small, relieved smile.

Nick put on a helpless, little boy face. 'Shouldn't you say "good" or something?'

'Should I?'

'Only if you think it *is* good. Do you?' There was a naked appeal in his eyes.

'Well . . .' Sarah began tentatively. 'If you were still going round with Clare, I'd think it was good . . .'

Gently, he took her hand. 'And if I were going around with you . . . would you think it was good?'

Her eyes met his stare. 'Yes. On balance, I think I would.'

Nick's hand gave hers a comforting squeeze.

Chapter 5

Confrontation

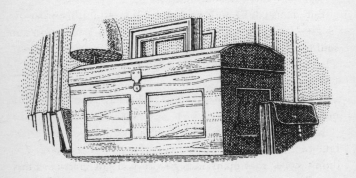

There was still nothing in it. Sarah knew that. She had only questioned Nick's marital status, she told herself, because Eleanor had kept whingeing on about it. And now that she knew the answer, Sarah was going to take great pleasure in telling her mother. She went straight up to Eleanor's flat on her return from meeting Nick. Maybe the news that he was unmarried would make the old bat shut up about him.

She should have known, of course, that that was a forlorn hope. Eleanor treated such topics as dogs do bones. They were endlessly to be licked at, nibbled and crunched; and if they ever appeared to be buried, it was only so that they could be dug up again later for further mastication.

Eleanor took the news calmly. 'I'm very glad to hear it, Sarah dear. There are so many totally unscrupulous men about.'

'Well, now you know that Nick's not one of them. And now I've put your mind at rest, perhaps you can allow me to get on with my own –'

'Oh, it's still not wholly at rest, you know.' Eleanor looked reprovingly at her daughter.

'Mother, there is nothing in it!'

But, as usual, Eleanor had a precedent to fit this situation. 'A girl I was at school with went out with a Venezuelan and said there was "nothing in it". She bore him seven children. Then *he* said there was nothing in it and went back to Caracas.'

Sarah sighed in exasperation. 'Mother, I can look after myself.'

Eleanor looked predictably dubious at this assertion. 'Just take care is all I say. You're vulnerable as well as Clare. You didn't know that many men before you got married. Emotionally, you're still very immature.'

'Thank you, Mother.' She put down her coffee cup, preparatory to leaving. If she stayed much longer, she was going to lose her temper. 'I can manage.'

'If you say so. But be careful. Just because you're a widow, you mustn't *gad*.'

'Mother, I am not gadding.'

Eleanor ignored the denial. 'Oh, it's a temptation. I found that.'

'But you were over seventy when you were widowed.'

Her mother looked affronted. 'No less temptation. Men still think you're fair game. Only three months after your father died,' she confided, 'Wallace Merton made a suggestion in his greenhouse.'

Sarah looked away, stifling the beginnings of a giggle.

'I said no, of course,' Eleanor asserted righteously. 'But it doesn't mean I wasn't tempted.'

Sarah rose. It really was time to go. 'No. Fine. Good. Well, look, I must be on my way –'

'Oh, incidentally,' said Eleanor as her daughter reached the door. 'Clare was looking for you.'

Sarah stopped in her tracks. 'Clare? Looking for me? That's unheard of.'

Eleanor fixed her daughter with a beady eye. 'She said she wanted a chat.'

'Oh no,' said Sarah, with an unpleasant sense of foreboding.

She didn't often go down to the basement, but that evening she suddenly felt an enormous urge to check through an old chest down there to see if any of the blankets in it would be good enough for the guest room.

However, that ploy only delayed the confrontation for half an hour. Then the door opened to reveal Clare, looking at her in some bewilderment.

'Mummy, what on earth are you doing down here?'

'Well, I, erm . . . I just wanted to . . . er . . .'

'I've been looking all over the house for you.'

'Yes, I, er . . . Well, as you see, I, er . . .'

'Mummy, I wanted to talk to you.'

Oh dear.

'About Nick.'

Hmm. Oh well, it had been nice while it lasted. And she'd known all along that it would end in tears. Even though, as she staunchly insisted to herself, there was nothing in it.

Clare misinterpreted her silence. 'You remember. Nick. That bloke you didn't approve of.'

'Oh yes,' said Sarah, as if dredging up some recollection from the ocean bed. 'Yes. I remember.'

'Well, I've stopped seeing him.'

'Yes, I know,' said Sarah without thinking. Then hastily she covered up. 'That is, I mean, I gathered.' She felt a tiny tickle of suspicion. 'When did you stop seeing him?'

'Last night.'

'Last night!' Sarah sat down heavily on the blanket chest.

'Yes,' Clare continued. 'I told him to get lost.'

'You did? Why?'

'He'd been two-timing me.'

'How do you know?' Again the instinctive response came out too quickly and had to be covered up. 'I mean, what makes you think that?' Sarah asked innocently.

'I heard about it from Sharon Wilson's boyfriend Miles's other girlfriend Tracey.'

Clare, thought Sarah, you do take after your grandmother.

'Tracey saw him in a pub. The Black Horse at Pelton.'

Oh dear. That had been the previous Tuesday. Sarah braced herself for the barrage of recrimination that was about to come her way.

'With this old woman,' Clare continued.

'Old woman!'

'Well, older than him, anyway. I was furious when I heard.'

Was it possible, Sarah wondered, that she really could escape, that she hadn't been identified? She crossed mental fingers as Clare went on.

'Pretty shabby behaviour, isn't it? Him making up to me and all the time he was going out with this prostitute.'

'With this – what on earth makes you think she was a prostitute?'

'Oh, come on, Mummy,' Clare replied brusquely, 'don't be naïve. Why else would someone like him want to go out with a woman as old as that?'

Sarah opened her mouth to remonstrate, to point out

that Clare was the one who was being naïve, that relationships between older women and younger men were quite possible and even satisfactory and . . . But she thought better of it. At the moment, incredibly, she seemed – though somewhat insulted – at least unidentified. She didn't want to put that precarious safety at risk.

'Anyway, that's not all,' Clare fumed on. 'I found out more than that.'

Oh. Maybe Sarah had been being over-optimistic.

'Lindsay Hackett told me. She got it from her cousin's fiancée's hairdresser.'

Yes, exactly like her grandmother. Sarah resigned herself to the worst. 'What exactly did Lindsay Hackett get?'

'The real truth of what Nick's been up to.'

'Oh. Tell me.'

Sarah wondered how she was going to cope with the inevitable eruption of anger. Clare was so completely in the right, and she was so completely in the wrong. It would be a sticky scene.

But what came next was not the anticipated fury. It was something else, something that took her completely by surprise.

'He's married,' said Clare.

'No, he's not!'

'He is. Lindsay Hackett's cousin's fiancée's hairdresser does his wife's hair.'

'Oh,' said Sarah flatly. And yet it wasn't a real surprise. In a way, she had always known, had willingly deceived herself.

Clare continued her damning evidence. 'Three children he's got. But he's always been unfaithful. Chats up anything in a skirt. He even had a fling with Lindsay Hackett's cousin's fiancée's hairdresser.'

'Really?' The fragile confidence of the last weeks seeped quickly away, as if it had never existed.

'So, anyway,' said Clare, 'I wanted to say sorry.'

Sarah was alarmed. 'Sorry to *me*? Why?'

'For not listening to you. You said he was probably no good.'

'Yes. Yes, I did.' The irony was almost as painful as the blow to Sarah's confidence.

Clare's face wore an expression of resignation. 'So go on, say it.'

'Say what?'

'I told you so.'

No, anything but that.

'Go on,' Clare insisted. 'Huh. You must be feeling pretty good at the moment.'

'Good?'

'Yes. You must be feeling really smug and self-righteous.'

Sarah gave her daughter a grin that was compounded of many emotions, though amusement was not one of them.

'Oh no, Clare,' she said ruefully. 'I wouldn't say that.'

Chapter 6

Restlessness

2.03. The red figures on the clock radio stared, unblinking and uncompromising, into Sarah's weary eyes. Digital clocks, she reflected, have made time so depressingly specific. In the good old days of clocks with hands, you could wake up in the middle of the night and not know what time it was. You could stay awake for a few, unspecified, elastic hours and, unless you took the trouble to switch a light on and look at your watch, you never had to define how long.

But those bloody glowing red squared-off figures destroyed all that. The display moved silently on to 2.04. Sarah had been awake for a whole minute now. And wide awake, with that raw, naked wakefulness that rules out the possibility of further sleep for at least an hour.

She contemplated taking a sleeping pill. She had had some in the first shock of Henry's death, and kept the supply constant with repeat prescriptions. But she fought hard to take them as rarely as possible, only when she was in a really bad emotional state. And she knew that by having one at 2.04, she would wait the best part of an hour for it to take effect, and then be woken by the alarm in the morning with a head stuffed full of kapok.

Sometimes a quick slug of whisky could relax her again. But she knew that on this occasion her mind was too active for it to have a quick effect. She'd need about half a bottle to subdue her. And that wouldn't do wonders for her head in the morning, either. Anyway, midnight drinking was another habit she didn't want to get into.

She saw the insomnia as another painful symptom of her widowhood. Surely she used to sleep better when Henry was there beside her? And yet she couldn't be certain. She had always slept well until she had Clare, and then she would have continued to sleep well but for the baby's disruptions. But those years disturbed the pattern; she never quite got back to that guaranteed, insouciant sleep she used to enjoy.

Yes, there had been wakeful nights while Henry was alive. Even so, they hadn't been as bad, had they? Surely? But again she couldn't be sure. His death had broken so many of the certainties of her life that now she had difficulties of attribution. She knew that she blamed her widowed state for problems that would have arisen anyway. It was impossible to prise apart cause and effect.

This familiar programme was instantly loaded in her brain. That was the depressing thing about waking in the middle of the night. Eyes open at 2.03, and immediately the mind was up and running.

She wouldn't have minded so much if it sometimes ran over a bit of unexplored ground. To be woken up by the excitement of new thoughts would, she imagined, be less aggravating. But, in her case, it was always the same ones, thoughts which had long since locked themselves into their own boring circles, as relentlessly irritating as a squeaking tumble-drier.

There were still the Henry thoughts, the predictable alternating cycles of loneliness and waste and regret and sheer fury at the unfairness of it all. The room didn't help when those cycles started. Though they had only been there together for a year, it was still the room they had shared. It was even the same bed.

That little thought-spiral always led straight on to the 'Should I move?' sequence and a tedious rehearsal of all the arguments for and against staying in a house so full of memories. Most of the time the question was of comparatively minor importance. Between two and four in the morning, like everything else, it loomed large.

And when she could derail her mind from those self-pitying grooves, the alternative directions in which it set off were equally dispiriting.

There was still the smart over her encounter with Nick, the dénouement of which had left her feeling infantile and stupid. God, she had behaved so immaturely! She winced at the thought of some of the things she had done, and, even more, at some of the secret things she had dared to think. Guilt about how she'd deceived Clare compounded her gloom. And always, at the back of her mind, was the unsettling feeling of having betrayed Henry.

Thinking of Nick led inexorably to another cycle of frustration, when she contemplated what had happened to her social life in the last two years. It seemed so arid. A lot of possibilities were barred by her new, unwanted status as a widow. All of the social contacts generated by Henry's work had been stopped, as if by a switch, the moment he died. And, because of the timing of the move from London, she was cut off from her old friends, without having built up a compensatory network of new ones.

Improving the situation just seemed to involve so much effort. She knew she should be positive, getting out and about, inviting people to dinner, joining societies, doing all the bright, active things recommended by smug little books on coping with widowhood.

But you needed confidence to do that. And Sarah's confidence had become a very unreliable resource in the last two years.

These thoughts led on to guilt over outstanding social debts. There were people she owed hospitality to. God, there was that hospital administrator, Clifford, and his wife Gwen, whom she and Henry had had dinner with just before the car crash. She really should summon up the energy to invite them back. It had been over two years ago now. Her recollections of Clifford and Gwen Davies as people were vague; they were just firmly lodged in her mind as an unpaid debt.

There were other people she ought to invite, too, other efforts she ought to make. It all seemed too much.

And always there remained one huge question, whose answer used to excite her, but which widowhood had made threatening.

How on earth was she going to get through Christmas?

She heard a sound from downstairs and tensed. When she had exhausted all other anxieties, there were always burglars and rapists to fall back on.

But no. Whoever it was was using a front-door key.

Clare. Sarah heard the soft padding of stockinged feet up the stairs and the discreet closing of a bedroom door.

2.37. The red figures offered their unblinking evidence. Why was Clare coming back at 2.37?

Yes, of course, even if Sarah forgot about burglars and

rapists, she always had her daughter and her mother to worry about.

Clare looked utterly washed-out when they met in the kitchen the next morning. She was gulping coffee, but Sarah decided not to reopen the 'proper breakfast' debate. Instead, she said in a neutral voice, 'You were in rather late last night.'

'I didn't make any noise,' Clare snapped.

'No, no. I just happened to be awake and I heard you come in.'

'If I didn't wake you up, then there's no need to criticize.'

'I wasn't criticizing,' said Sarah evenly, determined not to get into a slanging match.

'What were you doing then?'

'Just commenting.'

'Any comment,' said Clare, 'from a mother, implies criticism.'

Sarah still managed to keep her temper. 'All right then, I wasn't commenting. I was . . . observing.'

'Why?'

'What do you mean – why? Does there have to be a reason for everything?'

'I'd have said so. You must have had some reason for your "observation". Your telling me I was in late isn't news to me. I know I was in late.'

Sarah retreated before this volley of sarcasm. 'OK. OK. Sorry I mentioned it.'

'Next thing you'll want to know what I was doing,' said Clare truculently.

'No. I haven't asked, have I? I don't mind what you were doing. If you happen to want to tell me, then fine.'

It wasn't a total surprise that Clare didn't want to tell her. 'Oh, Mummy, I just wish you'd stop criticizing me for coming in late and disapproving of who I'm with all the time.'

'Disapproving of . . .?' Sarah couldn't believe her ears. 'Clare, have I said anything about who you were with? I didn't even know you were with anyone. And if you were, well . . . I don't care. It's none of my business. At eighteen you're old enough to decide who you . . . and it's hardly my place to . . .' Curiosity overcame her. 'Who were you with?'

'It's none of your business!'

No, it wasn't. Sarah regretted having started on that particular course. She tried a more conciliatory approach. 'I'm sorry, Clare, but if I'm awake at 2.37, I can't pretend I haven't heard you come in, can I?'

'Why were you awake at 2.37, anyway? Had *you* only just got in?'

'No, I hadn't.'

Clare slammed her coffee cup down on the draining-board. 'Oh, it's impossible living in this house!'

'What do you mean?'

'With you spying on me all the time.'

'I don't spy on you. It's just, if I happen to be awake at –'

'I really must move out.'

That took the wind out of Sarah's sails. 'But I thought, after that business with Nick, you –' Damn, even the mention of his name still made her look flustered.

'It's nothing to do with Nick,' Clare snapped. 'It's just common sense. Look, Mummy, if I were living in a flat, you wouldn't lie awake waiting to hear my key in the lock, because you wouldn't *expect* to hear my key in the lock.'

'No,' Sarah agreed doubtfully. 'On the other hand, I'd worry about whether you'd got back to your flat. And that'd be much worse, because I'd have no means of knowing whether you had or whether you hadn't.'

'Mummy!' Clare shrieked in exasperation. 'We must stop living in each other's pockets. I can't be accountable to you every hour of the day.'

'I'm not asking you to.'

'Yes, you are. Whenever I go out, you want to know where I'm going; whenever I come back, you want to know where I've been.'

'I'm just showing an interest.'

'I don't want your interest.' Clare enunciated the words very clearly. 'I want some privacy.'

Sarah knew her daughter had a point. She knew how furious she had used to get – indeed, still did get – with her mother poking her nose into everything. But then her mother was Eleanor Prescott, Special Investigator. Surely Clare couldn't think her own mother was as nosy as that? Could she?

'All right,' Sarah said. 'I understand. You've made yourself quite clear. I will not ask you any further questions about your movements. If there's anything you wish to tell me, I will in future wait until you volunteer the information.'

'Good. Thank you. I must be off.' And Clare made for the door.

'Where are you going?' The words were out before Sarah could stop them. 'I'm sorry.'

With one hand on the door handle, Clare turned and looked venomously at her mother. 'I am going,' she announced with icy precision, 'flat-hunting!'

Then she left, slamming the kitchen door after her.

Oh dear, thought Sarah. Well, I suppose I asked for that.

By the time she had got to work, she was feeling more positive. Clare's outburst had given a new stimulus to one of the circular debates of her wakeful night, and Sarah felt the time had come to make a few firm decisions.

Russell could sense that there was something she wanted to tell him, but it was not his method to ask her outright. He just let the conversation flow while he checked through the stock to see if there were enough books to justify a 'Romantic Novels for People with A-Levels' section.

Sarah, who was packing up mail orders for the post, told him about Clare's wanting to move out. And no, she said with the infuriating blush that even a tangential reference to Nick still prompted, she didn't believe there was a man involved this time. 'I think Clare just wants to get away from me.'

'I'm sorry,' said Russell sympathetically.

'Oh, don't be. I don't blame her. I can remember at her age I was desperate to get away from *my* mother. God, she used to nag me unmercifully.' Sarah shuddered at the recollection. 'But moving into flats just didn't seem so easy then. Anyway, Mother was determined not to let go of me. My liberation had to wait until I married Henry.'

'He was the US Cavalry riding over the hill?'

She grinned. 'He certainly was. And he arrived not a moment too soon. By then I had drawn my wagons into a tight circle and was running out of ammunition.'

'And what would have happened if you had run out?'

'Oh, Mother would have won. I would have stayed as her slave, looking after her in her old age.'

'Hmm. But with her in the flat upstairs, you are looking after her in her old age.'

'Mother would question that. She doesn't reckon my Help the Aged service is up to scratch. Anyway, she does retain a degree of independence . . . you know, separate entrance, that sort of thing. And,' said Sarah with a rueful smile, 'at least I did get away from her for twenty years, while I was married.'

'Do you think she'd really have liked you to stay around?'

'Oh, yes. I think all parents have a bit of that instinct to hang on to their children, to feel that their children can't manage the big world on their own . . . to prove, I suppose, that Mother knows best.'

'Do you have it?'

''Fraid so. Which is why it must be curbed. Why I must encourage Clare to get out and stand on her own two feet.'

'Very altruistic.'

'Not completely.' She punctuated the next sentence with staples as she sealed a jiffy-bag. 'It's part of something bigger.'

'Ah,' said Russell with relish, knowing that the real subject of the conversation was approaching.

'It's the house.'

'Thoughts of moving again?'

She nodded. 'That house is still full of Henry. I still sometimes look up and expect him to come in through the door. It's as if the walls are scrawled with the graffiti of our relationship. Not "Kilroy was here", but "Henry was here" – all over everything. I just think it might be better for me to try and make a new start somewhere where the walls are clean.'

Russell thought about this for a moment, then said judiciously, 'You don't want to rush into anything.'

'That's what everyone said straight after he died. "Don't do anything in a rush, Sarah. Give it time. Time is a great healer."' She snorted derisively. 'Well, I've given it time – two bloody years. And I suppose time is going through its healing process – though not quickly enough for my taste. God, time takes its time, doesn't it?'

'Famous for it,' Russell agreed with a sardonic smile.

'Anyway,' Sarah continued, building up a head of steam, 'I don't think if I moved now I could be accused of rushing into anything. And, if Clare goes, well, that could be just the stimulus I need. I mean, the house is far too big, even for just the two of us. If Clare went, I'd rattle round in it like a pea in a barrel. There's money, too,' she went on, fuelling her argument. 'Clare doesn't contribute a great deal, but it makes a difference. A house that size is far too expensive for me to keep going. I don't need all that space.' She took a deep breath before delivering her conclusion. 'No, I will go to the estate agents at lunchtime and put the house on the market.'

Russell looked up diffidently from a copy of *Rebecca*. 'Aren't you forgetting something?'

'What?'

'Your sitting tenant in the flat upstairs.'

Oh. Good point. In the rush of her thoughts, Sarah had got a bit ahead of herself. Russell's words didn't change her decision, but they did remind her of the need for tact and diplomacy in what she was proposing.

'Yes. Perhaps I had better have a word with Mother.'

Chapter 7

Tact and Diplomacy

'No, I understand fully, Sarah,' said Eleanor.

Her daughter was flabbergasted. She had steeled herself to this confrontation, anticipating all kinds of emotional blackmail and recriminations. She had boldly gone up to her mother's flat and, after the ritual of being provided with a cup of coffee, had boldly stated that, since Clare was thinking of moving out, it would be logical to sell the house.

And Eleanor had said she fully understood. She had taken it like a lamb. There must be something wrong with her. Perhaps she was ill. Senile dementia setting in . . .?

'Yes,' she continued, 'it's only to be expected that Clare should want to get away from you.'

Well, Sarah supposed that kind of line was only to be expected. Her mother was incapable of resisting the chance of a dig.

With a smile of infinite understanding, Eleanor expanded her point. 'If you don't mind my saying it, Sarah, you do nag her unmercifully.'

'Do I?'

'Oh yes, dear. It's one of the most difficult things for a parent to avoid, you know, nagging. But one has to try. I know. I was always rather proud of the fact that I never nagged you when you were younger,' she concluded with satisfaction.

The enormity of this was so great that Sarah was temporarily deprived of speech.

'It's all right, dear. You don't have to thank me. No, I fully understand your thinking about moving.'

'Good.' In spite of the sniping, this was proving easier than Sarah had dared hope.

'But,' said Eleanor, 'I have the solution to your problem.'

Oh dear. Maybe it wasn't going to prove so easy after all.

'What you must do is start to charge a proper rent for my flat . . .'

'But, Mother, you keep saying you're a poor old pensioner who can't possibly afford to . . .'

Eleanor overrode her, '. . . and let me move into Clare's room.'

'No,' said Sarah instinctively. No, a thousand times no.

'Why not? It seems to me an eminently satisfactory arrangement. You'd get the income from the flat and –'

'I'd also get you commenting every time I came in late.' Sarah didn't give her mother time to remonstrate. 'Listen, the only thing that keeps our relationship vaguely civilized is the fact that we have separate entrances. I know exactly what'd happen if we shared the same house. In a matter of days I'd have my wagons drawn back into a tight circle, and I think it'd be too much to hope for the US Cavalry to turn up a second time.'

Eleanor looked understandably bewildered. 'Sarah, what on earth are you talking about?'

'Never mind.' She tried to explain. 'Mother, my reasons for thinking of moving are not just financial. I actually want to get out of this house.'

This statement prompted an affronted 'Oh'.

'I need somewhere smaller, somewhere that doesn't remind me of Henry.'

'I see.' Eleanor had shifted instantly into Martyr Mode. 'And am I involved in these relocation plans?'

'Look, Mother, I haven't thought through all of the ramifications yet, but –'

'No. No, well, I suppose it would be too much for me to expect you to have done that. I see.' She moved into Stage Two of Martyr Mode, the Old People's Home Programme. 'Well, according to my friend Vera Poling, who lives in an establishment called The Sycamores, there are some very pleasant eventide homes around . . .'

'Mother . . .'

'. . . for elderly people who are beginning to become a burden.'

'All I'm suggesting is that we get the house valued and see where we stand and –'

But it was impossible to stop the programme once it had been started. 'Sarah, don't worry,' Eleanor went on, with a new frailty in her voice. 'I'll be all right . . . in some home where there's qualified nursing help available. I always think it makes sense for the elderly not to be sentimental, but face facts – and go into professional care rather than rely on the uncertain goodwill of their families. Don't you, Sarah?'

*

Russell got an action replay of this exchange the next morning. To give Sarah her due, she didn't force it on him. But he insisted on hearing all the grisly details. 'What you forget,' he said, 'is that it's a quiet, sedentary life being a bookseller. My only excitement comes from your reports of domestic mayhem.'

So Sarah gave him a quick rundown, concluding, 'She is just absolutely infuriating! She spends all her time going on about how glad she is to have her health, how glad she is that she can lead an active life . . . and then, the first moment there's a hint of anyone doing anything she doesn't want, suddenly she becomes bloody "elderly"!'

Russell chuckled. 'Did you resolve the situation at all?'

'No. I'm afraid on this occasion she had exactly the same effect on me as she has done ever since I can remember. I lost my temper. Up until then I'd been thinking, "Well, wherever I move, I must make sure there's room for Mother." Now I think the more miles we put between us, the better.'

Russell picked up the hint. 'You mean you're not thinking of moving locally.'

Sarah coloured. He was too quick for her. 'I don't know. I just want to live somewhere where I feel more sense of identity. Since I've been widowed, I seem to have lost sight of the real me. And living here doesn't help.'

'What do you mean?'

Slowly, Sarah tried to piece together what she did mean. 'Well, when we lived in London, I felt I had friends who I'd made in my own right. Quite a lot of them. There was another young mum called Janie. She was great.' Sarah smiled at the recollection. 'Really wild and disorganized. Always zooming round the house at high speed, bursting out of her dungarees, a dirty nappy in one hand, a saucepan in the other. Quite crazy. But fun in a sort of informal, relaxed way I haven't encountered with people down here.

'And there were a whole lot of other people who I felt were sort of close friends . . .' She racked her brains, but the names wouldn't come. 'Well, I suppose Janie was the main one, but . . . She was my sort of person. And she thought of me as *me*, not just half of "Henry and Sarah". But suddenly, when we moved down here, I became just "the doctor's wife".'

'You were the doctor's wife in London.'

'Yes, Russell, but not *just* the doctor's wife.' She gave a rueful grunt. 'Of course, now I'm not even that. I'm the doctor's widow. Utterly useless. Nobody sidles up to me at parties any more with confidences about their sciatica. They know there's no chance of my sneaking a nice quiet consultation with Henry about it.'

Russell reached down to put the kettle on. 'More coffee called for, I think.' As he sorted out the mugs, he asked, 'So do I conclude that you're thinking of moving back to London?'

What had seemed a certainty in the privacy of Sarah's mind became less definite under the beam of direct questioning. 'I don't know. It's a possibility. I'm sure I felt more *myself* there.' She sighed. 'Henry's death broke me into pieces and I'm still trying to reassemble myself. I still don't feel I'm all back together again.'

Russell nodded sagely. 'What doctors call "The Humpty Dumpty Syndrome".'

'No doubt. Feels more like a jigsaw to me.' As she spoke, she had a sudden, clear image from her childhood. 'I remember, when I was a kid, we had this big jigsaw of England, Wales and Scotland. Each piece was a county and you had to fit them all in.' The recollection became more vivid. 'You started from the outside, which was fairly easy because there was blue sea round the edges, but, as you got nearer the middle, it seemed to get more difficult. Or maybe some of the pieces had got lost, I can't remember. Anyway,' she concluded, 'I feel as if my edges have been fitted back together, but there's still something vital missing in the middle.'

'Like Leicestershire, for instance . . .?' Russell suggested.

'Yes. Or Rutland.'

As Russell spooned instant coffee into the mugs, he said, 'You have to remember, of course, that Rutland no longer exists. And some of the other counties have got new names. Humberside . . . Avon . . . Cleveland . . . Tyne and Wear . . .'

'Meaning . . .?'

'Meaning that things change. That you can't reconstruct the past.'

'No, not completely,' Sarah agreed. 'You can reconstruct bits of it, though.'

'You can try,' said Russell, without a great deal of confidence.

But the discussion was interrupted by the eruption of Clare into the shop. Her faced glowed with excitement, and she clutched a folded local newspaper in her hand.

Sarah greeted her with surprise. Although the building society was only a couple of streets away from Bygone Books, it was unusual for her to see her daughter during the day.

'Everything all right?' she asked with instinctive maternal anxiety.

'Yes. Great. Look!'

The newspaper was thrust in front of Sarah's face.

'What am I meant to be looking at?'

Clare's finger prodded at an advertisement. 'Lux. gd. fl. flt. 1 bdm. immac. cond. £21,500.'

'Great, isn't it?' Clare bubbled with excitement. 'Isn't it, Russell?'

Since he hadn't seen the advertisement, he restricted himself to saying he thought it might well be.

'Just a detail, Clare . . .' Sarah began tentatively, 'but have you got £21,500?'

'No, of course I haven't, Mummy,' said Clare, as if talking to an idiot. 'I'll borrow it.'

'Oh.'

'It's never too early to get one's foot on the first rung of the property ladder.'

Since Clare had started work, Sarah had noticed in her daughter a regrettable tendency to talk like a brochure when the subject of property came up.

'Look, love, I know you work for a building society, but there's no need for you to –'

'But don't you see – it's *because* I work for a building society that I can think of buying. Members of staff get special low-rate mortgages.'

'Do they indeed?' asked Russell in mock-seriousness.

'Yes. And the manager's very forward-thinking – really out to help first-time buyers.'

'Is he, by Jove?' asked Russell.

'He'll grant hundred per cent mortgages on suitable properties.'

'Well, well, well.'

'And he's always ready to listen to what you want and to give your case special attention – even if you're not a regular saver.'

'He's a saint. Not a man, a saint,' Russell murmured.

But Clare was far too excited to notice that she was being sent up. 'Anyway, I must dash. I fixed to view the flat at three. Just wanted you to see the details, Mummy.'

'Well, thanks,' said Sarah, as the newspaper was whisked out of her hands.

'Just a sec,' said Russell as Clare swept towards the door. 'Take this.' And he thrust a book into her hands.

'Oh, thanks. Must fly. See you.'

'But where is the flat?' Sarah called vainly to the closing door. She turned back to Russell with a grin. 'Well, at least one person's getting excited about the idea of moving.'

'Yes.'

'What was the book you gave her?'

'John Galsworthy. *The Man of Property.*'

'Ah.'

'Seemed appropriate, somehow.'

Clare was still full of the flat that evening, and went on about it at great length to her grandmother while Sarah prepared supper. Eleanor had been invited down to join them as a fence-mending exercise after the recent row. Food was a much-used currency for emotional transactions in the France household.

'It's a really great place, Granny,' Clare enthused. 'Only one bedroom, but quite big. And it's got use of this bit of garden. And if you stand up by the window, you can almost get a view of the park.'

'It sounds lovely, Clare darling,' said Eleanor a little too fulsomely.

Sarah gritted her teeth over the cheese sauce she was stirring. She knew that this excessive enthusiasm for Clare's plans was a statement about a certain lack of enthusiasm for Sarah's. Eleanor was highly skilled in using her granddaughter to get back at her daughter. Still, the object of the evening was to improve relations, so Sarah curbed her anger. Better show an interest. 'And you say the flat's down by the bus station, Clare?'

Her daughter wheeled round on her angrily. 'Mummy, for heaven's sake! Stop being a wet blanket!'

'What? Clare, I am not being a wet blanket. All I said was that the flat's down by the bus station.'

'Yes,' Clare agreed, 'but saying it's down by the bus station means, in your terms, that it's in a less salubrious part of town, that it's noisy, that there'll be lots of drunks and undesirables hanging round after dark, and that it's not the sort of area where you'd like your daughter to live.'

Sarah listened open-mouthed to this catalogue. 'Clare, you are putting words into my mouth and thoughts into my head. All I said was that the flat's down by the bus station. If that statement has any meaning other than the purely literal, then I should have thought it would be, "How very convenient for public transport."'

'Not the way you said it,' Clare mumbled truculently.

'I didn't say it any particular way. I just said it. Look, if you have misgivings about where the flat is, fair enough. But don't put them into my mouth.'

Eleanor decided that she had been silent too long. 'Clare wasn't putting anything into your mouth, Sarah. And there's no need for you to take that line. I know it's just sour grapes.'

'Sour grapes?' Sarah stopped stirring the sauce.

'You're jealous of Clare's youth, and you're jealous of her independence.'

'Am I?'

'Yes. You wish you'd had the gumption to set up on your own when you were her age.' Eleanor turned to her granddaughter with a smile of complicity. 'Goodness, Clare, I kept encouraging her to get out into her own place, but would she listen? Oh, no, she insisted on staying around at home.'

Sarah tried to speak, but words wouldn't come.

'No, Clare, I had to wait till your father came along to get rid of her.'

Sarah found her tongue. 'Mother, we seem to have very different recollections of that period of our lives.'

'It's only to be expected. The young always romanticize. Oh, and, look, dear, I think that sauce is burning.' Sarah turned back in fury to the cooker, while Eleanor continued her private conversation with her granddaughter. 'I'm really delighted about the flat idea, Clare. You're just at the age when you should be doing this sort of thing. You see,' she went on wistfully, 'you can move at will. It's not as if you have any responsibility to anyone else in making your plans.'

'Meaning that I have?' came a snarl from the cheese sauce.

Eleanor looked across at her daughter in innocent surprise. 'Sarah, you are putting words into my mouth and thoughts into my head.' Then she gave her granddaughter the full beam of her smile. 'Incidentally, Clare, if you do need to borrow some money for moving expenses, fitting the place out, that sort of thing, I do have a little tucked away.'

'Thank you, Granny.'

'I thought you were a poor old pensioner,' Sarah objected in disbelief. 'You keep saying you're incredibly hard up.'

'There's hard up and hard up,' her mother replied serenely. 'I am not well off, but when I hear a case of genuine need . . .'

'I see.' Sarah reached a dish of stuffed pancakes out of the oven and poured the cheese sauce over them. As she did so, she asked gently, 'And the money is going to be all right, is it, Clare? I mean the mortgage.'

But once again her concern was misconstrued. 'Mummy, don't start again.'

'Start what?'

'Putting a damper on the whole thing.'

'I wasn't. All I asked was whether the mortgage was going to be all right. A perfectly innocent inquiry. Can't I say anything without being misinterpreted?'

'It's not what you say,' Eleanor interposed, 'it's how you say it.'

Sarah put the pancakes in the oven to heat up and closed the door with considerable force. 'Well, look, just assuming – and I know it may be difficult for you to make this assumption – but just assuming that my question was posed from a standpoint of genuine interest and nothing more, could you tell me, Clare, if you have got your mortgage sorted out?'

'I'm going to see him tomorrow,' came the surly reply.

'Who?'

'The manager.'

Ah, Robin Hood himself, thought Sarah. Out loud, she asked, 'And you're sure you've budgeted for the actual costs of moving, solicitor's fees and –?'

'You're doing it again,' said Clare venomously.

'What?'

'Trying to bring me down.'

'I'm not.'

'Yes, you are,' said Eleanor.

'No one asked you, Mother. Look, Clare, all I'm doing is asking. The kind of mortgage you're talking about sounds to me to be pretty huge, given what you earn, and –'

'Oh, stop being so pussyfooted!' Clare snapped. 'You're always so pussyfooted about money.'

'I just don't want you to get into difficulties.'

'Will you let me make my own decisions?' her daughter stormed.

Sarah worked very hard to keep her temper. 'Yes. Just so long as you're aware of the ramifications of those decisions. You're at an age when you should be doing lots of other things with your money apart from paying off a mortgage. You should be travelling, having holidays and –'

Clare rose to her feet. 'Oh, for God's sake, Mummy! Shut up!' she shouted. And she swept out of the kitchen, slamming the door.

'Clare, what about your supper?' Sarah called forlornly after her.

There was a long silence.

Inevitably, Eleanor was the one who filled it. 'Well, congratulations, Sarah. I think it's very sad when one sees the enthusiasm of the young dampened by the cynicism of the old.'

Sarah reached for some plates from the rack and put them to warm. 'Thank you, Mother. Particularly for the word "old". Much appreciated.' No, no, must stop this sniping at each other. In a more reasonable tone, she continued, 'I just don't want Clare to take on more than she can cope with.'

'You don't want her to move away from you.'

'It's not that. It really isn't. I just want her to be fully aware of the kind of financial burden she's taking on. I mean, even with a preferential mortgage rate, she's proposing to borrow a lot of money. That's all I'm worried about. All right?'

'All right,' Eleanor conceded. But it was not in her nature to leave the subject there. Casually, she said, 'I hope you've been into how much it's going to cost *you*, if you go ahead with your plan of moving.'

'Yes, thank you, Mother, I have,' replied Sarah, tight-lipped. 'It'll cost me about £5,000. Fortunately, at the moment I have more than that in the deposit account, and, anyway, since one of the main purposes of moving is to go somewhere cheaper, the expense will not be a problem.'

'Good. I just wanted to be sure that you had thought it through.'

'Well, I have!' Sarah snapped. But no, control the temper. Try and be nice. The aim of the supper was, after all, to make up for the last row – mustn't let it lead to another one.

'Mother,' she said in a gentler voice, 'when I talk of moving you mustn't think that I'm not taking you into account.'

'Oh no, dear. I don't want you changing your plans because of me.'

Sarah saw the signs of Eleanor moving back into Martyr Mode. I must keep my temper, I must keep my temper, she thought as she began, 'Mother, what I mean is that, anywhere I go –'

'Just don't think about me. Please.' The Martyr Mode was

now firmly locked in. 'I mean, after all, moving is a long process. Who knows, by the time you actually get it all sorted out, I may have conveniently . . . slipped away.'

'Mother . . .'

'And, even if things don't work out that well, I'll still be all right. I rang Vera Poling yesterday to ask for details about this place where she lives. The Sycamores. It sounds very nice . . . for an elderly person.'

Sarah could feel the anger mounting within her. 'Listen, what I meant was –'

'No, you mustn't worry about me,' Eleanor continued imperturbably. 'You just go ahead and sort out your life. And leave me to sort out . . . what's left of mine.'

This was too much for Sarah. 'Oh, for God's sake, Mother! Shut up!' she shouted. And she swept out of the kitchen, slamming the door.

'Sarah, what about your supper?' Eleanor called forlornly after her.

Chapter 8

Going Back

Sarah felt disproportionately excited about being on the train. It was so easy. London was only an hour and a half away. An off-peak day return was really very reasonable. Why on earth didn't she do it more often?

She had a precarious sense of independence. Maybe this would be the new pattern of her life . . . going out to lunch with friends, being more active socially, being a person in her own right. And somehow she knew that that kind of independence would be easier to achieve if she lived in London.

But the moment she had shaped this new image, guilt again sidled into her thoughts. It was the old ridiculous feeling of betrayal, that by changing too much she would in some obscure way be letting Henry down. She knew it was nonsense, but it seemed an inescapable accompaniment to any surge in her confidence.

Still, never mind. Don't make long-term plans. One day at a time. And this day promised to be an enjoyable one. Janie had sounded really pleased to hear from her, delighted at the prospect of meeting for lunch. And Russell had created no problems about her taking the day off. Indeed, he had encouraged her. He had noticed her restlessness of the previous few weeks and was keen for her to do anything that might allay it.

So, yes, it should be a good day. She'd have time to look in a few estate agents before she met Janie. Then a nice, really self-indulgent lunch. Yes, full three courses, plenty of wine, a bit of real pampering, like those very rare, treasured binges they used to snatch when they had offloaded the children on friends from playschool. Lots of time to catch up on everything with Janie. Lovely.

She snuggled into her train seat and looked luxuriously at the expensive magazine to which she had treated herself.

Sarah had suggested they should meet in an Italian restaurant which had been a favourite haunt for celebrations when she and Henry had lived there, but Janie had said the place had changed hands 'and gone down terribly'. Her alternative proposal was a new wine bar, which she said 'everyone was going to'.

Of course, that only meant everyone local; it was hardly one of the fashionable eateries of Central London. As she walked along the parade of shops towards it, Sarah was reminded how village-like the area was. When she talked of 'London', what she really meant was this inner dormitory suburb, some twenty minutes by fast train to Waterloo.

Being there again, she was more struck by the similarities

to where she now lived than by the differences. Similar sort of houses, similar sort of shops. Just everything closer together. And noisier. She had forgotten how busy that main road was. And she had completely forgotten about the aeroplanes which passed overhead every minute on their way to Heathrow.

The wine bar was very new, white tiles everywhere, dark brown tables and chairs, a lot of big potted plants which looked too perfect to be anything but plastic. Waiters and waitresses, in those shin-length white aprons made fashionable by the brasserie boom, scuttered about with long menus and salvers of drinks held shoulder-high.

It felt unnaturally warm inside after the early October chill of the street. Sarah peered around at the clientele, which looked depressingly young, a bit brash and rather overdressed. They were all talking loudly and confidently. There was no one she recognized.

She supposed it was silly to have expected it. She had just thought that, having lived there for over ten years, she would have seen a few familiar faces. But that was ridiculous. It was a suburb with a quickly changing population, where young successful professionals tended to buy their first house and breed a couple of babies before moving to larger houses further outside the metropolis.

Apart from the lack of other familiar faces, there was no sign of Janie. Sarah looked at her watch. Oh well, she must have got there first. Punctuality was a provincial virtue; maybe she'd been away from London too long.

She was looking round, trying to catch one of the swooping waiters to show her to a table, when she was distracted by a woman on the other side of the room who appeared to be waving at her.

It couldn't be. Surely? Sarah's recollection of Janie was of someone chubby and amiably scruffy, rushing round the house cooking meals and mopping up after children, dressed in variegated dungarees and smocks more remarkable for their flair than their elegance. Her straw-coloured hair had always been scraped back into rubber bands, and her vivacious face innocent of make-up. The effect had been enormously vigorous and attractive, but hardly *soignée*.

And yet the woman trying to attract her attention was dressed in a sharply cut dark blue suit with fashionably square shoulders. As Sarah moved in a state of semi-hypnosis towards her, she also noticed that the stranger had copper-red hair cut in an immaculate helmet shape, and shiny make-up outlining the contours of her cheekbones. Her eyelids boasted three separate colours.

And she was *thin*!

Janie looked more like a heroine from an American soap opera than the earth-mother of Sarah's recollection.

Half-way through her half-bottle of Sancerre (Janie had insisted she would stick to Perrier), Sarah began to relax. There was nothing really daunting about her friend, in spite of the glossy new image. She caught little glimmers of the old slapdash character peeping through the cracks in Janie's veneer. And those elements were as endearing as ever.

Janie's sophistication dropped away as she started giggling helplessly at the recollection of a fancy-dress party which they and their two husbands had attended.

'It was at the Pringles's, wasn't it?'

Sarah caught the infection of the giggles. 'That's right. Goodness, Janie, I'd completely forgotten about that. But it's coming back.' She giggled more as she recalled the occasion.

Their waiter arrived. Just a green salad for Janie. The new-found thinness was clearly maintained at some cost.

And an earthenware bowl of lasagne for Sarah. A rather small bowl, she observed. She wished she'd had the nerve to order some of the delicious-looking garlic bread, but she'd felt guilty when her friend was being so ascetic.

Still, on with the conversation. 'Yes, I remember now – I went to that party as a trifle. Had a huge plastic cherry on top of my head.'

'Did you? I don't remember that. I know that Henry had gone as a gladiator and then his bleeper went and he had to go to the hospital in his breastplate and tunic.'

This prompted another paroxysm of mutual giggling, at the end of which Janie whipped out a small mirror to check her make-up.

But the giggling and the one, undressed lettuce leaf which had passed her lips appeared to have caused no lasting damage. She put the mirror away again and sighed. 'Oh, he was a great character, Henry.'

Sarah nodded.

'Everyone really missed him when you moved.'

Sarah nodded again, more soberly.

'Well,' said Janie with a giggle, 'he was the only doctor in the practice who spoke English.' Then, feeling perhaps she ought not to ignore Sarah's bereavement, she continued, 'Of course, you must miss him a lot, too.'

'Yes. Yes, I do.'

'Such a character. People still talk about him.' As she spoke, Janie's eyes were busy, looking round the wine bar, maybe expecting to see someone else she knew.

'Do they talk about me, too?' asked Sarah tentatively.

'What? Talk about you? Oh, yes. Yes, of course. You *and* Henry. They talk about both of you. As a couple.'

It wasn't quite the answer Sarah had hoped for. Still, on with the reminiscence. 'It's funny, thinking back to the Pringles's fancy-dress party. That was such a silly evening.'

'It was,' Janie agreed. 'Of course the Pringles have moved now.'

'Have they?'

'Yes. He got posted to Abu Dhabi.'

'Ah.' Sarah tried to wring something else out of the famous evening. 'It was that same evening that the Chattertons went to dressed as a knife and fork.'

'That's right,' said Janie. 'They've moved, too, actually.'

'Oh.'

'Well, the children were off their hands and they decided they needed a smaller house.'

Sarah shook her head in disbelief. 'Goodness, I can't believe that their children are old enough to –'

'Both the girls are married.'

'Really?'

'The Chattertons will be grandparents in the spring.'

'Gosh, that makes me feel old.'

'We *are* in our forties, Sarah,' said Janie reprovingly. Then she preened herself, as if mentally adding, Not of course that I look it.

'Yes, but even so . . .' Sarah began. And then, feeling a little chastened, she said another, quieter 'Yes.' She scraped round her bowl for the last bits of lasagne. It really had been rather small, positively mingy, compared to the portions at the Red Cow at Stipton. This wasn't one of those restaurants that got away with meanness on the excuse of *nouvelle cuisine*, was it? Not with lasagne, surely?

She wondered if Janie would disapprove very strongly if she ordered an apple strudel. No, maybe better not.

Sarah chuckled as another recollection came back to her. 'Tell me, how are your lunatic neighbours, the Simmondses? Do the kids still think you both own both houses? Do you still have that permanent babysitting arrangement with them?'

Janie looked at her as if she was mad. 'Sarah, my youngest child is sixteen. He hardly needs babysitting.'

'No, no, of course not. Sorry, I wasn't thinking.' Sarah was suitably subdued. 'How are the Simmondses, anyway?'

'They've moved.'

'Have they?'

'Yes. Dick got made redundant and they've gone out to manage a sub-post-office in a remote village in Wiltshire or somewhere.'

'Oh.'

'So they've ended up in the country, like you.'

'Oh, come on,' Sarah remonstrated, 'I'm hardly in the country. I live in the middle of a town of some fifteen thousand inhabitants.'

'Yes, but I mean it's all the same, isn't it? It's not London.'

With a shock, Sarah realized that three years before, she might have said just the same thing. She remembered the insularity of people in London, the inability to believe that any sort of life could exist outside, the conviction that anyone who claimed to enjoy living away from the capital must be covering up some secret inadequacy.

'Well, I'd hardly say . . .' But there was no point. She'd just sound defensive. And Janie wouldn't understand, anyway. Better to start a new subject. 'So you've got new neighbours then?'

'Yes.' Janie grimaced. 'I'd hoped we'd get another couple with kids when the Simmondses went, but it was not to be.'

'So who are they?'

Janie made an even longer face. 'Not "they" – "she".'

'You don't make her sound much fun.'

'She isn't,' said Janie. 'A widow, and all that that entails, if you know what I mean.'

The tactlessness was so blatant and enormous that it couldn't have been deliberate. There was no point in being offended. With a quiet smile, Sarah said, 'I know what you mean.'

Janie suddenly realized her gaffe. 'Oh,' she said, 'Sorry.' And she looked at her watch.

Chapter 9

A Possible Solution

Russell looked up at the sound of the shop door opening. Not a customer, surely, just before closing time. But no, it was Sarah, standing somewhat sheepishly inside the shop in her smart going-up-to-Town coat, fingers twitching slightly at her going-up-to-Town handbag.

'Well, this is a surprise. I thought you were enjoying the bright lights of London.'

She smiled wryly. 'They gave me a headache.'

'Too bright?'

'No. Just too . . . too long ago perhaps.' She put her hand-bag down on a table and hovered, as if uncertain whether to stay or go home.

'And did you look at any property?' asked Russell.

'I went into a couple of estate agents before lunch.' She made a face. 'God, the prices, though. For what I'd get for the house here I'd be lucky to get somewhere half the size.'

'You have to shop around,' said Russell judiciously.

'Yes. I was all set to spend the whole afternoon going to more estate agents, but, I don't know . . .' She sighed. 'After lunch I felt too dispirited.'

'So how was Janie?' The question was posed lightly, almost without intonation.

'Oh, fine.' Sarah took off her coat and flopped into a chair. 'Just made me realize, though, how special that part of one's life is, when you're all young couples with children, when the children's needs are your first priority. It makes you get very close to people with whom you may not really have a great deal in common.'

There was a long silence before she revealed the final insult. 'What was really unnerving was the fact that Janie was *thin*.'

Russell shook his head in mock-horror, as Sarah stood up and said briskly, 'Anything happened here? Anything that needs doing?'

'At half-past five on a Thursday?' Then, in a gentler voice, he asked, 'Why did you come, Sarah? Why didn't you go straight home?'

She shrugged. 'I suppose I just wanted to tell you that you were right.'

'How very gratifying. About what in particular?'

'I went off today looking for Rutland and Radnorshire and Cumberland and Kirkcudbrightshire . . .'

'And what did you find?'

Sarah grinned. 'Oh, you know . . . Humberside . . . Avon . . . Cleveland . . . Tyne and Wear . . . Gwent . . .'

*

Clare was sitting at the kitchen table with her head propped up in her hands, the picture of abject misery.

'What on earth's the matter, love?' asked Sarah the minute she came into the room.

Clare burst out crying and instantly shed about ten years. It was just like those days when she had come back from school with the terrible news that her Best Friend was now Best Friends with someone else and they weren't letting her be in the Gang any more.

Sarah reacted just as she had always done, and sat down beside Clare, with her arms round her daughter's shoulders. And, as always, slowly and jerkily through the tears, the story came out.

Someone else had made a cash offer on the flat, and it had been accepted.

Once again her daughter's immaturity was driven home to Sarah, the huge gulf between the surface sophistication and the defenceless childishness which could so quickly show through the smallest crack in that surface.

'I'm sorry, love,' she soothed. 'But these things do happen. House purchase is like that. There are lots of disappointments. You build up these massive fantasies about somewhere and then they get demolished. Oh, come on,' she continued in a jollying voice, 'there are plenty of other flats.'

'Not ones that I could afford,' said Clare mournfully.

'But, surely, if you could have afforded that one . . .'

'Ah.'

There was a wealth of meaning in that monosyllable. 'You mean you couldn't have afforded that one?'

'I saw the manager this afternoon,' said Clare with resignation.

'The great philanthropist himself.'

'Yes. Except his great philanthropy didn't extend quite as far as I'd hoped.'

'Oh, dear. You mean you don't get a preferential mortgage rate?'

'Oh yes, I do. Or I will. But I haven't been long enough in the job yet to qualify.'

Sarah gave her daughter another hug. 'Oh, love, I'm sorry.'

'And then, when he heard how much I was proposing to borrow, I got this huge lecture about costing, and cutting one's coat according to one's cloth and not taking on too big a commitment and . . .' Anger was now taking over from self-pity. 'God, he was so pussyfooted! He made your attitude to money sound positively reckless.'

This was about as near as Sarah ever got to a compliment from her daughter, so she said, 'Thank you.'

Clare blew her nose noisily, as if to put the crying firmly behind her. 'So, anyway,' she said, a hard, defensive note creeping into her voice, 'the upshot is that nothing can happen for some time. You and I are stuck for a few more years getting on each other's nerves.'

'You mean with me waiting up every night till I hear your key in the lock?'

'I suppose so.' Clare gave a gesture of despair. 'Oh God, I might be reduced to having to get married, like you did.'

Sarah took a deep breath. That was her cue, and she was unlikely to get a better one. She had a proposal to put to her daughter, an idea she had worked out on the train back from London. But she'd have to be careful. Building bridges to Clare was not always a successful manoeuvre, and their relationship was littered with half-finished ones for which her daughter had refused to build the other half. Still, it was worth a go.

'There might be another solution, Clare.'

'What?' The question was discouragingly aggressive.

'Listen – and hear me out, please, before you give any reaction. Look, you know we don't use the basement –'

Clare ignored her mother's request to hear her out. 'Yes, but if you're suggesting I move down there, it wouldn't make any difference, because we'd still be in the same house and use the same front door and still be living in –'

'Wait till I've finished! What I am suggesting is that I should have the basement converted into a flat.'

'A flat?'

Sarah pursued her advantage. 'Yes. I've got enough money in the deposit account to afford it. I get it converted into a flat . . .'

'With a separate entrance?' asked Clare warily.

'With a separate entrance. You pay me rent, a realistic rent, but something you can afford, and we can each lead independent lives.'

Clare worked it out slowly. 'So Granny'd be in the flat above, and me in the flat below? Like a sandwich?'

'With me as the fish paste, yes,' Sarah agreed wryly.

'And you wouldn't check what time I came in at night?' asked Clare, intrigued, but still suspicious.

'If the conversion's done properly, I wouldn't *hear* what time you came in at night.'

'So you wouldn't move? None of us would move?'

'No.' There was a silence. 'What do you think of the idea?'

Clare jutted forward her lower lip dubiously. 'I think it *could* work. Possibly. Perhaps.'

Sarah knew that that was as positive a reaction as she was likely to get, and pressed on. 'So do I, Clare. Possibly. Perhaps. Enough to give it a try, anyway. And it would be a great weight off your grandmother's mind to know that we're not moving.'

At that moment, as ever judging her entrance to perfection, Eleanor opened the door and walked into the kitchen. Like her daughter, she was dressed up in her smartest clothes. Clearly, she, too, had been out visiting.

She sailed into the room and sat down at the table, tossing gracious greetings to her family.

'Mother, excellent timing, as usual,' said Sarah, and went on eagerly, 'Clare and I have just worked out where we are going to live.'

'Good.' Eleanor smiled a complacent smile. 'I've worked out where I'm going to live, too.'

'Oh?'

'I've just come back from visiting Vera Poling. At The Sycamores. A delightful haven for the elderly. A charming lot of residents. Very nice class of person. Some real gentlemen. One of whom, I have to confess,' she chuckled coyly at the recollection, 'did get a little fresh. But quite charmingly, I hasten to add. I've always rather favoured the older man. No, I think I could be very happy there.'

'Mother,' said Sarah, when she could finally get a word in, 'I'm not moving.'

'Aren't you, dear?'

'No. Nor's Clare.'

Eleanor looked quizzically at her granddaughter. 'No?'

'No.'

'Oh.' She let the silence stay for a second, then went on with great satisfaction, 'So it'll just be me then, will it? Visitors are welcomed at The Sycamores every day, there's twenty-four-hour qualified nursing help and –'

Sarah tried to interrupt. But in vain.

'No, I'm really looking forward to it now. I think it could be a very stimulating environment for someone of my age. A lot of like-minded people in a similar situation, also abandoned by their families. I think –'

'Mother,' said Sarah firmly, 'will you stop that?'

'Sorry, dear?' Eleanor gave her daughter a charming smile. 'Was there something you wanted to ask me?'

Of course. It was never Eleanor's style to give in easily.

She would wring the last drop out of this, as she did out of everything else. Sarah would have to go through all the hoops of begging.

No point in dragging it out. Better stomach my pride and give her what she wants straight away, thought Sarah. 'Yes, Mother. There was something I wanted to ask. Would you like to stay in your flat upstairs?'

Eleanor couldn't have asked for more abject supplication. But still she revelled in her power, and extended the scene. With another guileless smile, she said, 'Well, Sarah . . . I'll tell you what, dear. I'll think about it.'

Chapter 10

Trust

Sarah knew she was quite capable of making decisions on her own. While Henry had been alive, because his work as a GP took so much of his energy, she had been left to make many of the major domestic decisions. And yet he had always been there to talk to, to tell what she had decided, to act as a kind of confirmation for her actions. So their decisions, if not exactly mutual, were at least shared.

But now she missed having him there as a sounding-board. Though on her own she probably made just the same decisions as she would have done while Henry was around, she now felt less secure about what she had decided, had more misgivings, woke up more often in the night wondering whether she had taken the right course.

And there was really no one else who could fit into this consultative role of Henry's. Sarah knew that her mother would give her eye-teeth to be involved in every one of her daughter's decisions, but Eleanor was quite nosy enough already and did not need that kind of encouragement. Also, she was a very strong-willed old lady and decision-making could quickly become a contest between them rather than a constructive process of discussion.

Clare wasn't a lot of use either in that respect. There was in her a hard line of selfishness, partly due to her age and partly to the self-protective screen she had built up around her since her father's death. She would monitor carefully any decisions that concerned her directly, but maintained a pose of indifference to everything else.

And Russell, dear Russell, was a wonderfully ready ear for far too many confidences already. Sarah knew it really wasn't fair for her to take advantage of him further by involving him in her domestic decision-making process.

No, once again, as she had discovered with renewed shock so many times over the last two years, she was on her own.

The major decision she had made recently – to convert the basement into a flat for Clare – she felt confident about. It did seem a sensible solution to their various domestic and financial problems.

And it wasn't going to be too big an undertaking. There was a bit of a damp problem to be sorted out, but nothing serious. A proper front door would have to be made, a bathroom and kitchen plumbed in, but otherwise the bulk of the job would be just decorating.

So that major decision Sarah knew to be the right one. But it was all the minor decisions that followed on from it which caused her anxiety. In particular, there was the problem of who she should get to do the job.

The house, when the Frances moved in, had been in good

rcpair and as a result they hadn't required the services of a builder. 'In the fullness of time' they would have turned their attention to the basement and, even if Henry's exotic ideas of saunas had not materialized, they would certainly have converted the space into individual studies for the two of them. Of course, as things turned out, Henry was not granted 'the fullness of time'. And so Sarah had no useful precedent to rely on in her search for a builder.

Asking around in the town produced variable responses. For every glowing recommendation of an individual builder there was a horror story of some job he had botched. Local builders all seemed to be magic figures, around whom an apocrypha of disasters gathered, and it was very difficult to sort out the truth from the mythology.

But the decision had to be made. The job needed doing. And, in the cause of domestic harmony, it needed doing as soon as possible. Ideally, in the next couple of months. Somehow the great threat of Christmas would seem less if Clare had her own flat. The more circumstances were different, the less direct comparisons could be made with Christmases when Henry was alive, then maybe the more tolerable (or less intolerable) the festive season would be.

Ultimately, if she was ever going to find a builder, Sarah just had to take a shot in the dark. So she did all the right things, rang a selection of numbers from Yellow Pages, got a series of estimates, and chose the builder who gave the most reasonable quote and who, she had feebly to admit, 'seemed the nicest'.

From the moment she had committed herself, the misgivings began, and in the small hours of the Saturday morning before the Monday when he was due to start work, she lay awake agonizing for a long time.

As a result, she was tired and scratchy over breakfast

coffee in the morning, and she questioned the wisdom of inviting her mother down to join her. This was a Saturday morning habit she had got into, a little ritual, like Sunday lunch, to try to give a feeling of family solidarity.

But that morning, with Eleanor at her infuriating brightest, and Clare at her equally infuriating grumpiest, Sarah wondered how good an idea it was.

Still, have to make the best of it. She attempted communication with her daughter. 'Did you have a good evening, Clare?'

This elicited no response.

'*I said*, did you have a good evening?'

Clare mumbled something that could have been 'All right', and that had the intended effect of angering her mother.

'Clare, I asked a civil question. It is very ill-mannered not to give me a civil answer.'

'I am not good in the mornings,' Clare growled.

'I am not good in the mornings, but at least I try to be polite.'

Eleanor beamed. 'I'm good in the mornings.'

'No one asked you, Mother,' Sarah snapped, instantly failing in her aspiration towards morning politeness. She turned back to her daughter. 'So . . . what did you do yesterday evening, Clare?'

Again, there was no response. 'I see.' Sarah picked up the paper and said sarcastically, 'Well, I hope you won't think me ill-mannered if I read, but if you're not going to talk . . .'

'I'm quite happy to talk, Sarah dear,' said Eleanor perkily.

'I don't think we're reduced to that, Mother.' Sarah wished she could have curbed her tongue, but she was just too tired.

She looked at the paper, whose front page was rich with lurid allegations from the latest sensational murder trial. 'I see the Red Scarf Strangling case is still going on,' she observed. 'More evidence from the mistress. Hmm, I wonder how long he'll get.'

'If he's convicted,' Clare grunted.

'What do you mean – *if* he's convicted?'

'He hasn't been found guilty yet.'

'No, but I mean, Clare –'

'The British legal system is based on the premise that everyone is innocent until proved guilty.'

'Yes, I know that, but in this case . . . I mean, there's no question. All the evidence points to him.'

'There might be a perfectly innocent explanation,' Clare continued doggedly. She wasn't arguing for any reason other than perverseness. She was in a mood to disagree with her mother on principle. And to make digs at her. 'Just because you've got a suspicious mind –'

'Listen.' Sarah spelled it out, itemizing the points on her fingers. 'He was in love with the mistress, he hated the wife, the wife wouldn't give him a divorce. He admits to driving the wife out to the chalkpits, where she was found next morning strangled with her own scarf. His fingerprints were all over everything, traces of her blood were found under his fingernails. And just because I suggest he might be guilty, you say I've got a suspicious mind.'

'There could be another explanation,' Clare insisted.

'Huh. You read too much Agatha Christie.'

Clare maintained her attack. 'Anyway, that's only one example. You do have a suspicious mind.'

'Do I?'

Eleanor wasn't going to miss a cue like that. 'Yes, you do, dear.'

'Oh,' said Sarah wearily. Sometimes she could cope when the two of them ganged up on her. At other times, like now, she found it very difficult. 'Can I ask how my suspicious mind manifests itself?'

'It manifests itself all the time,' Clare replied. 'It manifests itself in you asking me what I was doing yesterday evening.'

'Why? Did you do something I should be suspicious of?'

This question seemed to Clare only to prove her point. 'See what I mean? You always think the worst of everyone, you always distrust people's motives.'

'I do?'

'Yes, you do, dear,' said Eleanor, maintaining the two-pronged attack.

Sarah tried to justify herself. 'Now listen, you can't go through life being too gullible. You have to be a bit wary, a bit circumspect with people, otherwise they take advantage of you.'

Clare shook her head pityingly. 'I find it very sad to hear you say that, Mummy.'

'Oh?'

'Yes. If you take trust out of human relationships, what is there left?'

Eleanor endorsed her granddaughter's opinion. 'Exactly.'

'Will you stop agreeing with her?' Sarah snapped.

'Why shouldn't I agree with her?' asked Eleanor innocently. 'She's right. Trust is the basis of all human relationships.'

'Yes, maybe, but –'

'And, Sarah, you really should try to curb this suspicious instinct that you have.'

'Mother, I –'

But Eleanor was not to be deflected. 'Just because you're a widow, there's no need to get *crabby*.'

'Crabby?'

Clare joined in again. 'Yes, that's exactly the word.'

Sarah sighed. When the two of them joined forces, it was very exhausting. 'Thank you,' she said. 'I see. And I owe this "crabbiness" to having been widowed, is that it?'

'Yes,' said Eleanor, and then reconsidered. 'Well, no, not completely.'

'Thank you.'

'No, you always did have a suspicious streak.' And, as ever, Eleanor had a precedent to draw from her quiver of reminiscences. 'I remember, when you were three, you thought the little boy next door had stolen your Smarties.'

'Well, he had.'

But this perfectly reasonable justification was inadequate for Eleanor. 'That's not the point. A nice child wouldn't have had the suspicion in the first place. And I must say,' she went on, 'this tendency has been worse since you were widowed. Henry was a good influence in that way. He did dilute your natural sourness a little.'

'"Natural sourness" now, is it?' Since they had clearly set her up in the role of Aunt Sally that morning, there wasn't much point in offering resistance.

'Yes,' said Eleanor.

'That's right,' Clare confirmed.

'Look, I don't have to sit here and have you two insult me.'

'We're not insulting you, dear,' Eleanor explained in a kind voice.

'No? You could have fooled me.'

'No, dear. This is just part of the give-and-take of family life.'

Sarah grunted. She had had enough of her mother's specious definitions. 'Well, whatever it is, I can do without it. I just thought, Saturday morning, we can all have a nice cup of coffee together. Another time, Mother, you can stay in your own flat.'

'Oh, I would, dear. Quite happily.' Eleanor smiled complacently, before launching into one of her regular routines. 'If only my little kitchen-diner weren't so depressing. That wallpaper . . .'

Sara sighed and gave the regular response. 'I know,

Mother, and when I've got some money, I'll have it decorated.'

Eleanor sniffed. 'It needs rather more than decoration.'

'Yes, but at the moment all my spare cash is going into having the basement done and –'

'Oh, I know, dear, I know. Don't worry about me,' said Eleanor nobly. She left a little pause before starting on yet another of her regular routines. 'Anyway, there's not much point in brightening up a place for someone who probably won't be around for very much longer . . . is there?'

Sarah resolutely refused to rise to this.

Deprived of the stimulus of reaction, Eleanor changed tack. 'No, I'm delighted to think that Clare will soon have her own flat.'

'So am I,' said Clare with feeling.

'So am I,' said Sarah, with even more feeling.

'The builder starts Monday, does he, Clare?' Eleanor inquired.

Why did she ask that? thought Sarah. She knows full well he starts on Monday. Hmm, time to be wary. Her mother was working towards something in her usual devious way, but Sarah didn't yet know what it was.

Clare confirmed that the builder was indeed due to start on the Monday, and Eleanor said that it would be a relief to get the work under way. 'What was his name again, Sarah?'

'Terry.'

'And remind me – how did you get on to him? Was he recommended?'

Ah. Sarah saw what she was up to now. Her mother was starting to niggle about the choice of builder, about the fact that she hadn't been consulted in that choice. She would try to drive a few more wedges of doubt into Sarah's already deeply uncertain mind.

'No,' Sarah replied breezily. 'I just had to take pot luck.

Still, Terry does seem to be awfully obliging. And looks very honest. Got these big brown eyes. What's more,' she continued, trying to convince herself as much as her mother, 'his estimate was way below the others. Most of them seemed to just think of a number and double it. Terry really went through it all, though. Seemed actually to be thinking about the job from my point of view. He decided eventually my cheapest way was going to be to pay for the materials myself and then pay him by the hour for his labour.'

'You see, dear,' said Eleanor with a sweet smile, 'there are people around who can be trusted. You must learn to give people the benefit of the doubt.'

'Yes. Yes, of course. I do.' A little ripple of uncertainty crossed Sarah's mind. 'I hope he'll be all right.'

'What do you mean?'

'Well, Mother, he did seem very pleasant, but you hear some terrible stories. There seem to be such a lot of cowboys about.'

Clare looked up from her coffee cup. 'You're doing it again, Mummy.'

'What?'

'Thinking the worst of people.'

'No, I –'

'Yes, you were, Sarah dear,' Eleanor agreed.

'Look, will you both stop –'

'You know, Mummy . . .' Clare began ruminatively.

'Yes?'

'If I were ever to get accused of any crime . . .'

'Hmm?'

'I hope to God I wouldn't get landed with anyone like you on the jury.'

Oh, her daughter could be a little charmer, couldn't she?

'Thank you, Clare,' said Sarah.

Chapter 11

Suspicion

In the small hours Sarah was awake again, twitching, fretting about all kinds of silly worries, which she knew in the morning would shrink back to their proper proportions, but which at night loomed grotesquely large.

Was she really capable of making decisions like this one about the builder without Henry's guidance? Would Terry turn up on time? Was he any good? Was he a cowboy? Was he going to take advantage of her gullibility just because she was a woman on her own?

And did the fact that all these circular suspicions were racing through her head mean that her mother was right and she really was becoming 'crabby'?

At least one of her anxieties was allayed when, on the dot of eight o'clock in the morning, Terry arrived to start work on the basement. And he seemed as friendly and open, and the big brown eyes seemed as honest, as on their first meeting.

So, once she had given him a key and made him a cup of coffee (and warned him that any strange noises from upstairs were not burglars but her mother), Sarah set off for work in a considerably more cheerful frame of mind.

Her mood was improved further when she remembered that the day's programme was not just a usual Monday in the bookshop. Russell was attending a book auction and had invited her to go with him. So that would mean a nice drive through the country, the excitement of the auction itself, and, knowing Russell, a pub lunch somewhere. A good day out, in fact. A day to take her mind off builders and suspicions about incipient 'crabbiness'.

They drove through countryside in which the trees looked as if they needed one more breath of wind to strip them completely and take away their last pretence that it wasn't winter. British Summer Time had ended on the Saturday night and, as always, the year seemed to have taken a quantum leap into the gloom. Christmas and all that that entailed loomed menacingly close.

In spite of her intentions, it didn't take long for the conversation to home in on Sarah's family. This wasn't because she forced the subject on Russell, but because he retained his inexhaustible curiosity about everything that went on in the France household. His own home life with Bob was so cosy and placid that, he often said, he needed the stimulus of hearing about Sarah's. As he once put it, 'You realize, without your accounts of domestic mayhem, I'd have to go back to watching *Dallas*.'

So she gave him a brief account of the pincer movement from mother and daughter that she had suffered on the Saturday morning.

At the end he chuckled. 'Sounds to me as if they were just sending you up.'

'Oh yes, they were a bit. I know they were. They do sometimes gang up on me. And sometimes I feel strong enough to cope with it. And sometimes I don't.'

'And just now you don't?'

'Exactly.' There was a silence as she looked out at the bleak, bare farmland. 'I think perhaps what really worries me is that they might be right . . .'

'That you don't trust people?'

'Yes. That I actually *am* becoming sour and suspicious.'

Russell dismissed the idea. 'Can't say I've noticed it.'

'I think it happens to everyone a bit . . . you know, as you get older. You sort of . . . lose your *naïveté* about people. Maybe you get hurt once or twice . . .'

'Like you did with Nick?'

'Oh, I wasn't meaning anyone specific.' Sarah was furious to find that even now the mention of the name and the recollection of her own stupidity brought a flush to her cheeks. 'All I mean is that suddenly you find you're no longer looking at the world as if you were Little Noddy.'

'Did you ever?'

She sighed. 'I don't know. I can't say, really. I mean, I've changed so much in the last couple of years . . . you know, since Henry died . . . and I can't sort out which changes would have happened anyway and which are a direct result of being widowed.'

'I don't see why being widowed should make you suspicious of *people*. Henry was killed in a car accident, due to mechanical failure. No one was directly to blame.'

Sarah tried to explain. 'It goes deeper than that. His death just hit my confidence so much, I felt there was no longer anything I could trust or believe in. I mean, if Henry could just suddenly go like that, then anything could happen. For the first year, it was as if all the world had gone into negative – everything I had relied on as white was suddenly black, and all the blacks were suddenly white.'

'I know, Sarah,' said Russell quite firmly, 'but you're over that first shock.'

'Oh, sure.' She grinned. 'Yes, most of the time the colours are back to normal. And when they're not, I now know my moods well enough to be able to twiddle the controls and get a reasonable picture back. What I can never decide, though, is whether the picture I get these days is as good as the picture I used to get.'

Russell could never resist following through that kind of image. 'Of course, it may not just be the picture. It may be that the programmes you're receiving now aren't so good. The standard of television has dropped off badly over the last couple of years,' he observed sardonically.

'So what should I do?' asked Sarah, keeping the bubble of the idea afloat. 'Keep re-running all my old videos of life with Henry?'

Russell was suddenly serious. 'No. Just try not to be making comparisons all the time.'

'Good advice.' She smiled wryly. 'Hard to follow. I suppose what really frightens me is the thought that I've lost control of my life.' She let out a little primal scream of frustration. 'God, I hate being a widow! Not so much because it means I've lost my husband, but because of all the implications that the word carries. If I'm introduced to someone as a widow, they immediately make a whole load of assumptions about me, assumptions which I resent deeply – and it's quite possible that I resent them so deeply because some of them are true. Maybe,' she concluded mournfully, 'I really am becoming crabby.'

'Crabby?' Russell echoed curiously.

Oh yes, of course, he didn't know. 'My mother's latest charming description of me.' Another wave of frustration seized her. 'Oh, it's horrible how things fester when you're on your own! A couple of years ago, if Mother had called me "crabby", I'd just have said, "Silly old cow – it takes one to know one", and never given it a second thought. Now I find I wake up at five o'clock in the morning worrying about it.'

'Not just about that?'

'No. You name it, I worry about it. This morning I was in agonies about whether this builder was going to turn up or not.'

'But he did?'

'Oh yes. On the dot of eight. Seems very keen and willing and conscientious.'

Russell shrugged. 'You see. Your fears were groundless.'

'I suppose so. And now I feel rather awful about having been suspicious of him.'

'He'll be all right. Don't worry,' Russell reassured her. 'Look, he's given you a price – all he'll want to do is to get the job done as quickly and efficiently as possible.' He chuckled. 'No, the builders you have to be careful of are the ones who charge hourly rates. If you're not there all the time, watching them like a hawk, that type are usually off doing other jobs.'

The van was drawing into the auction-room car-park as Sarah murmured, 'Oh dear.'

'What's the matter?'

'Russell,' she sighed, 'I'm afraid suddenly you've got me feeling all sour and suspicious again.'

The rest of the day was as pleasant as she had anticipated. The auction was not only enjoyable but also productive. Russell got very excited about two lots in particular, which he reckoned would justify two completely new sections in the shop – 'Cookery Books Containing Recipes You Might Actually Cook' and 'Fantasy Literature That Avoids Being Twee'.

They had the hoped-for long lunch in an almost deserted pub, and were back at Bygone Books late in the afternoon. Then they started making room for the new sections, and sorted through the rest of their prizes.

As a result, it was nearly six-thirty when Sarah got back home. She had been too preoccupied all day to dwell on her anxieties, and it was only as she put her key in the lock that she remembered the building work on the basement should have started.

So the first thing she did after removing her coat was to go down through the door in the hall to see what progress had been made.

To her surprise, she found that the lights were on. Oh dear, she'd have to have a word with Terry about switching them off. But, worse than that, as she looked round, she could see very little evidence of any work done. The piles of furniture and rubbish in the back room looked exactly as they had in the morning. Not a thing moved.

Oh well, maybe there'd be some progress in the front room, the one Clare had designated her bedroom. Sarah pushed the door open.

There again the light was on. And in the middle of the room stood her daughter, holding a tape measure.

'Clare. I didn't expect to find you down here.'

'I was just planning. You know, working out where I'm going to put everything when the flat's ready.'

'Ah. So *you* put the lights on, did you?'

Clare looked at her curiously. 'Yes. I can't see in the dark. I'm not a cat, you know.'

'No, no, of course not.' One relief, anyway. Wouldn't

have to take Terry to task about the lights. On the other matter, though . . . the front room showed no more signs of work started than the back one had.

'Anyway, why did *you* come down here?' asked Clare.

Her expression was guarded, almost suspicious. Sarah felt inappropriately guilty and said the first thing that came into her head. 'Oh, I, er, just came to see if Terry wanted a cup of tea.'

Her daughter tutted. 'Honestly, Mummy, it's after half-past six. He started at eight o'clock this morning. You can hardly expect him still to be here.'

'No. No, of course not.'

The suspicion had not left her daughter's eyes. In fact, it seemed to have intensified. 'You sure you weren't coming down to check up on him?'

'What, me? Goodness. Would I . . .? No.' But, in spite of her denial, Sarah couldn't help being worried by what she saw – or, rather, what she didn't see – in the basement. 'Mind you, looking round, there doesn't seem to be much evidence of a great deal of work done today.'

'He probably had to go off and buy materials and things.'

It was a perfectly reasonable explanation. Sarah wished she could be completely convinced by it. 'Yes, yes, I suppose so . . .'

'You gave him some money to do that with, didn't you?' asked Clare.

'No. He's going to get all the stuff and then give me the bills.' Sarah was struck by a new anxiety. 'He hasn't given me any bills yet.'

Clare let out an exasperated sigh. 'Mummy, give him a chance. It's only his first day.'

Her mother looked up for reassurance. 'So you don't think I should worry?'

'No. Of course not. Just trust someone for once in your life.'

Oh dear. Back to that. Sarah supposed she had really asked for it.

'Terry's a perfectly honest and reliable workman,' Clare continued, 'so there's no need for you to get all . . .'

Sarah held up her hand with resignation. 'Don't say it. Crabby? Am I right?'

'Yes,' said Clare.

Sarah wished she knew more about building. The next two mornings Terry appeared on the stroke of eight, and the next two evenings when she got back from work, she went down to check what had happened in the basement during the day. Each time there was some evidence of work – dust-sheets shifted around, a little plaster removed – but not much. Maybe this was a necessary part of the preparation for the job and maybe it had kept Terry busy all day. Or maybe he was taking her for a ride. Sarah wished she knew enough to be certain.

She didn't dare to confide her suspicions to her mother or daughter. She had had quite enough of their strictures on the crabbiness of her nature and didn't wish to give them any further cues.

And she tried not to burden Russell with her worries. But, on the Thursday morning, while they were cleaning pencil marks off some of the children's books they had got at the auction, he asked her directly how things were going on the flat conversion.

She tried to minimize her anxiety for his benefit, but he wasn't fooled. 'So you really do think he's cheating you?'

'I just don't know.' She sighed. 'What makes it so awkward is that he's such a nice lad. I feel terrible for harbouring these awful suspicions of him. He's got these great big brown eyes that look terribly vulnerable.'

'I dare say Judas had great big brown eyes that looked terribly vulnerable,' Russell observed unhelpfully.

'Thanks very much. You really know how to set a girl's mind at rest.' She sighed again. 'The trouble is, I'm getting paranoid about it. I just seem such a classic target for a conman. Widow, out at work all day, fairly ignorant about this sort of thing, used to husband dealing with that side of life, too genteel and middle-class to want to make a scene – any cowboy worth his salt'd see me coming a mile away.'

'And what evidence do you have so far that this Terry is a cowboy?'

'Nothing positive. Just suspicions. I mean, as I say, not much work seems to be getting done.'

Russell made a rueful face. 'Sounds as if he could be off doing another job.'

'Yes, he *could*. Or this could just be necessary preparation work that I wouldn't understand about.'

'Hmm.' Russell blew the pencil rubbings off a page and examined the book critically through his half-glasses. 'If he is working on another job, of course, the question is – are you paying for it?'

'What do you mean?'

'You'll have to wait and see what hours he says he's put in on your basement. If he claims that he's done a full week, then he probably is on the fiddle.'

Sarah groaned inwardly at the thought.

'What's he going to do?' asked Russell. 'Give you hour-sheets?'

She nodded. 'We've fixed that each Friday he'll give me a list of his hours and I'll pay him accordingly.'

'What about the materials?'

'He'll give me bills for those at the same time.'

'So . . . on Friday all will become clear.' Russell shrugged, without great optimism. 'Of course, there's another thing to watch.'

'What?' Sarah asked weakly. She didn't think she could cope with *another* thing.

'Materials,' he replied gloomily. 'Some of these cowboys – and I'm not saying Terry *is* a cowboy – but some of them don't only get a client to pay for their time on another job, they also charge him for the materials.'

'What do you mean?' asked Sarah feebly.

'I mean that you must scrutinize all the bills he gives you very closely. If there's anything there that you can't match with your requirements, then you know you're being done.'

'What sort of thing?'

'Well . . .' Russell spread his hands wide as he searched for an example. 'Say he presents you with a bill for five hundred metres of thirty-five millimetre copper piping . . .'

'Yes?'

'And the job you've asked him to do could not possibly require five hundred metres of thirty-five millimetre copper piping . . .'

'Which it certainly couldn't.'

'This is only an example, Sarah,' he said reprovingly. 'But say that did happen, then you'd know that either your builder was making you pay for another job . . . or he'd suddenly taken up modern sculpture. Either way, you'd be being done.'

'Yes. And if I discovered I was being done, then there would have to be a major confrontation.' It was the one thing she had dreaded from the moment the whole business started.

'I'm afraid so,' said Russell. 'Mind you,' he went on, offering what comfort he could, 'under those circumstances the procedure would be simple. You just wouldn't pay him.'

Sounded easy. Sarah tried to imagine herself face to face with Terry, looking into those big brown eyes and refusing to pay his bill. Her imagination couldn't quite cope with the image. 'Oh dear,' she sighed. 'It does seem terrible to have to be so suspicious.'

'No point in being cheated.'

'No.' Russell was right, no question about it. She had embarked on this course, and she would have to see it through. 'I suppose it must be easier if you're at home all day. Then you can at least keep an eye on people you've got working for you. Spy unobtrusively, see what they really get up to.'

'Don't forget,' Russell reminded her, 'that you have got your own built-in spy in the house.'

She looked at him, puzzled.

'Your mother still lives upstairs, doesn't she?'

'That's true.'

'And from what you've said of her, she seems not to be without a certain aptitude for espionage.'

Yes, of course. Russell was right. Sarah had spent her entire life trying to keep out of the range of her mother's hypersensitive antennae and trying to curb Eleanor's congenital nosiness.

But, if her mother was actually *asked* to be nosy, actually given a licence to snoop . . . why, she'd be in seventh heaven.

Sarah didn't do anything about it straight away. She wanted to extend the benefit of the doubt towards Terry for as long as possible. When she saw his work-sheets and his bills on the Friday evening, then she'd know whether he was cheating her or not.

The next two days passed slowly and anxiously, but at last she was home after work on Friday. Her handbag was bulging with ten- and five-pound notes drawn from the building society to pay Terry's bill.

It was just before six. That morning the builder had turned

the beam of his big brown eyes on her and said that he'd stay till six. And he'd leave the paperwork on the hall table for her to check through.

It was there, as promised. Sarah looked at it warily as she took off her coat. She was tempted to have a drink before she confronted the truth, but curbed the instinct. No, she must face this unaided.

From downstairs she could hear Terry whistling cheerfully as he tidied up in the basement. The noise sounded so innocent, it made her feel even guiltier. Still, appearances could be deceptive. The work-sheet and the bills would tell all.

She steeled herself, picked them up, and looked through them.

Then she looked through them again.

But no, she hadn't made any mistake. Terry claimed to have put in forty-three hours' work in the house that week. And there were bills for wallpaper and kitchen units that she had certainly not ordered.

Sarah felt a cold trickle of anxiety in her stomach.

The major confrontation she so feared could no longer be avoided.

Chapter 12

A Major Confrontation

Sarah sat in the sitting-room, building up her resolution. She had Terry's work-sheets and bills on the table beside her. Her handbag was there, too, swollen with its building-society booty. But Terry, she was determined, wasn't going to get any of those ten- and five-pound notes until he'd offered a few explanations.

Sarah felt slightly sick. She hated this sort of thing, always had. A wave of misery swept over her. She felt so on her own. Why wasn't Henry there to shield her from this burden? Why wasn't *anyone* there? It wasn't fair.

But no, that was no way to think. She had fought for two years to keep self-pity at bay, and she wasn't going to give in to it now. She must be very positive. Yes, that was it, positive. She wouldn't succumb to middle-class diffidence and embarrassment. She wouldn't listen to any flannel. She would avoid looking into the big brown eyes. She would say what she had to say with firmness and dignity.

Think what Henry would have done, that was the line. Yes, how would Henry have played the scene?

A little sliver of doubt pierced her mind. She had a sneaking feeling that Henry would have felt as awkward about the situation as she did. He hadn't been particularly good at this sort of thing either, and in fact he would probably have tried to duck it as much as she did. But somehow it had been different when there were the two of them. Neither had had that much instinctive confidence, but together they had managed to bolster each other and survive.

This maudlin circle of thought was interrupted by a tap on the door.

'Come in,' said Sarah in a voice that came out uncomfortably loud.

'Ah. Terry,' she continued, as if any one of a hundred people might have been tapping on her sitting-room door at six o'clock on a Friday afternoon.

He grinned. His grin was horribly disarming. And those big brown eyes did look so honest and innocent. Sarah stared fixedly down at the floor. She was going to go through with this. She gestured to a chair.

'I won't sit, thanks, Mrs France. Overalls probably a bit dusty. Don't want to do for your nice chair-covers, do I?'

Oh dear. He wasn't making it any easier by appearing so solicitous. Sarah steeled her resolution by looking at the bill for kitchen units. She *hadn't* ordered them. However good his manners were, Terry was definitely taking her for a ride.

'You got the work-sheets, I see, Mrs France.'

'Yes. I, er, yes.'

'I didn't take the full hour off for lunch every day, but I've treated it like I did . . . you know, kept the hours down as much as possible.'

'Oh, thank you,' Sarah found herself saying. 'That's very good of you.'

There was a silence. 'No problems about anything?' asked Terry.

That was a cue, if ever there was one. Sarah took a deep breath. 'Well, er, um . . . well, just one or two . . .' This was not the positive, forthright approach she had intended. 'I mean the, the items . . . some of the items on these bills . . .' she continued lamely.

Terry shook his head in rueful sympathy. 'I know, wicked, isn't it? The prices they charge for this sort of stuff. I mean, obviously I get all the discount I can, but even so . . . Actually,' he confided, 'I haven't charged you for the emulsion. Got some left over from another job, so I used that.'

Eleanor's genteel upbringing of her daughter did not fail. 'Oh,' Sarah heard her voice say. 'That's very kind.'

'Think nothing of it.' Terry chuckled. 'If you can't do a fellow human being a good turn every now and then, what's life for, that's what I say.'

Sarah found herself laughing in agreement, and made the fatal mistake of looking up into the big brown eyes.

'So,' said Terry, 'I think the total was £337 . . .'

'It was, yes.' Unbidden, her hands were reaching to undo the clasp of her handbag and extract the bundle of notes. Equally unbidden, they were counting out £337.

'Say £330 for cash,' Terry continued.

Again he got the Pavlovian response of politeness. 'Oh, that's very decent of you. I did go to the building society and get this lot out, but I . . .'

Unaccountably, Sarah's hands were now proffering the

bundle of notes towards Terry. He took them with a cheery 'Thanks', while Sarah's tongue lay paralysed in her mouth.

He handed a few notes back. 'Go on, you take the seven. I insist.'

'Oh, thank you,' Sarah's voice said. 'Are you sure?'

'Yeah.'

This was becoming ridiculous. She snatched her stare away from the big brown eyes and began to remonstrate. 'Look, I don't think you should just take the money and –'

He held up a pacifying hand and winked. 'Don't worry, Mrs France. I won't bother to count it. I know when I'm dealing with someone I can trust.'

'But, Terry –' she continued in desperation.

'Don't say another word,' he said amiably, as he started for the door. 'Have a good weekend, Mrs France. See you Monday.'

Oh dear, thought Sarah, as the door closed. I'm sorry, Henry.

Chapter 13

Espionage

The non-confrontation with Terry left Sarah feeling wretched and useless. There was no way round it, she had failed dismally. She had shown herself to be spineless and ineffectual. Whatever her occasional hopes of living an independent life, she had now demonstrated unarguably that she was quite incapable of managing on her own. She was not only being taken for a ride by a cowboy, she was also voluntarily paying her fare.

All these tedious, cyclical thoughts, needless to say, went through her mind in the small hours of the Saturday morning. She wished she could be a bit more fixed in her opinions. She wouldn't even have minded a touch of bigotry. Here she was, unquestionably being ripped off by Terry, and yet her mind was still trying to find excuses for him, still hoping that she had misinterpreted his actions, still trying to bend logic to make everything all right. Dear God, who did she want to be – Little Noddy?

But eventually sleep came back. And she didn't wake again till after eight in the morning (no alarm set on a Saturday). As ever, things didn't seem quite so grisly in daylight.

And life had to go on. So she went off to do the week's shopping.

It was in the 'canned fruits' aisle at Sainsbury's that she suddenly remembered an idea Russell had mentioned. Yes, before staging another (and hopefully more successful) confrontation with Terry, there was something else she could try. A way of double-checking on his activities. To give her final proof of his perfidy. She would put the idea into practice as soon as she got home.

The new thought made her feel more cheerful. She treated herself to a can of lychees.

It stood to reason, really. If someone has devoted her entire life to nosiness but always met with disapproval from people who don't find nosiness an admirable quality, how wonderful it must be for her suddenly to be asked – nay beseeched – to channel her nosiness in a useful direction.

That was what was going through Sarah's mind as she waited on the little landing outside her mother's flat. Eleanor seemed to be taking her time, so Sarah knocked again.

This time her mother appeared. But she only opened the door a crack and her manner was rather flustered.

'Mother. Everything all right?'

'Yes, Sarah dear, of course. Hello.'

'I wondered if I could just have a word . . .?'

'Of course, dear. Any time.' But she made no move to open the door any wider.

'Can't I come in?'

'I'm sorry, better not. I've, er, just burnt a pan of milk on the stove. There's smoke everywhere.'

That would explain her mother's confusion. Eleanor prided herself on keeping every square inch of her flat spotless. She wouldn't want Sarah to witness even the smallest kind of domestic accident.

Not that it mattered. The conversation could just as well take place on the landing.

'Actually, Mother, I wondered if you could do something for me . . .?'

'Of course, dear. Anything.'

'Listen, it's about Terry . . .'

Eleanor smiled with approval. 'That nice young builder, yes.'

'That young builder, anyway,' said Sarah wryly. 'Look, I'm afraid he may be taking me for a ride.'

'Oh, surely not. He seems so obliging.'

'Conmen always are obliging – that's one of their skills.'

'Conmen?' her mother echoed.

Sarah explained. 'I'm worried that he's cheating me over the hours he's putting in here.'

Eleanor looked suitably shocked at the idea, so Sarah came to the point. 'Look, it's almost impossible for me to check up on him when I'm out at the bookshop all day, so I was wondering whether you would mind . . .'

'What?'

'Just keeping an eye on him, seeing how long he stays here, seeing what he actually gets up to.'

Eleanor stared at her daughter in pained disbelief. 'Am I to understand, Sarah, that you are asking me to spy on him?'

'Exactly. Yes.'

A long silence was allowed to elapse before Eleanor responded, and when she did, it was not with the reaction that her daughter had expected or hoped for.

'Sarah, I am shocked. Not only shocked that you should think me capable of doing something so deceitful as spying on a fellow human being . . .'

Sarah protested, 'Oh, come on, you've spent your entire life –'

Eleanor overrode her majestically. '*But also* shocked by yet more evidence of your suspicious nature. Sarah,' she continued, now more in sorrow than anger, 'I too have been widowed, but I think I can say, without undue modesty, that I have never allowed myself to become . . .'

Sarah resigned herself. 'Yes, I know. Crabby.'

'Yes,' said her mother severely.

This new battering from Eleanor was quickly followed by another from Clare. Even when not actually working together, the two of them had an uncanny instinct for coordinating their attacks.

Clare found her mother in the kitchen, putting away the morning's shopping. She walked in with a very purposeful and righteous air.

'Mummy.'

'Yes?' said Sarah without turning round. She was trying to fit a large pack of frozen sweetcorn into a freezer compartment which seemed to have shrunk.

'Have you been down to the basement recently?'

'Yes. Well, I mean, not since yesterday evening, but –'

'And have you seen what's happening down there?'

'Yes, Clare.'

'Or rather what's *not* happening down there. Look, it's a week he's been in this house now, and there's absolutely nothing to show for it down there.'

'No.' Sarah squashed the sweetcorn in and pressed the freezer door shut.

'Well, what's going on?' asked Clare resentfully. 'He's obviously a crook.'

Sarah turned to face her daughter. 'Oh, come, come, now. That doesn't sound like you. I thought you were always recommending me to think the best of people.'

Clare sighed with exasperation. 'Mummy, there's a difference between thinking the best of people and being plain gullible.'

'I see. So I'm gullible now as well as crabby – is that it?'

'Yes,' said Clare, as if this had been stating the obvious. 'I mean, Terry is clearly just a cowboy.'

This so closely echoed Sarah's growing conviction that she felt bound to deny it. 'There might be another explanation. Remember, Clare, trust is the basis of all human relationships.'

But Clare's avowed principles did not get in her way when her own self-interest was under threat. 'Never mind trust, Mummy,' she almost snapped, 'we're talking about my flat. I've ordered kitchen units and everything to be delivered in a fortnight, and at the current rate of progress, the place just isn't going to be ready in that time.'

Sarah agreed glumly. Then she clutched at a straw of comfort. 'You say you ordered kitchen units?'

'Yes.'

'You didn't ask Terry to buy them for you?'

Clare looked bewildered. 'No, certainly not. Why do you say that?'

Another hope dashed. 'Oh, I was just trying once again to think the best of people. And once again unfortunately failing.'

'Never mind that,' said Clare brusquely. 'You must give Terry a good talking-to.'

'But I'm never here,' Sarah objected. 'That's half the trouble. I haven't time to talk to him when I'm out at work all day.'

'You must *make* time,' Clare insisted implacably.

Sarah was beginning to get a bit sick of this. What right had her daughter to speak to her as to an irresponsible child? Clare was the one who was going to benefit from all this, after all.

'Why don't *you* make time? As you keep saying, it's *your* flat.'

Clare dismissed the suggestion with contempt. 'Yes, I know it'll be my flat. But I'm not paying the bill. You are.'

'Oh, I see. And that gives me the privilege of dealing with any problems that may arise?'

But Clare had inherited her grandmother's deafness to irony. 'Of course it does, Mummy,' she replied, again as if explaining to a small – and not particularly well-behaved – child. 'Don't you understand – that's what responsibility means.'

Sarah turned away in fury. The freezer door swung open, and the pack of sweetcorn fell out at her feet.

Having steeled herself over the weekend to the prospect of 'having it out' with Terry, Sarah found that once again, come the Monday morning, her resolution was trickling away like the moat of a sandcastle.

He arrived again right on the dot of eight. And once again he seemed so cheerful (though, if he was doing what Sarah suspected he was doing, he had every reason to be cheerful). And once again the big brown eyes looked almost childishly innocent and vulnerable.

And once again Sarah chickened out and set off for work in a state of mounting self-hatred at her feebleness.

Russell, whose project for the day was amalgamating the 'Socialist Studies' and 'Political Thought Lightly Tinged with Marxism' sections into one 'Left-Wing Books that are Actually Interesting' section, quickly detected that she was ill at ease. As quickly, he deduced the cause of her uneasiness.

And he had a solution immediately ready. 'I reckon the only thing you can do is to spy on him yourself.'

'Oh dear,' said Sarah, who had been fearing that suggestion.

'Yes. Take tomorrow off. I can spare you here.' He gestured ironically to the shop, whose customary vacancy remained unchallenged. 'The book trade seems to be going through yet another lull. Then you can see for yourself what Terry actually does with the day. Lurk around the house and watch.'

Sarah made a face. 'I don't think I'm very good at lurking.'

'I don't see that you have much alternative,' he said with a shrug. 'If you don't think you can engineer a confrontation without more positive evidence, and if neither your mother nor Clare's going to help you out . . .'

'Which they're certainly not.'

'Then you'll just have to watch him for a whole day yourself and find out what he does. Clock him in when he arrives . . .'

'But he's always very punctual about that.'

'Yes, but you must see how long it is before he goes off to work on another job. Actually count the hours he does with you, and then find out whether there's anything to show for it at the end of the day.'

Sarah saw an objection straight away. 'Isn't he going to think it odd if I keep popping in to check up on him?'

'Oh, you mustn't do that. You mustn't let him know you're there.'

'No?'

'No. That's what I meant about lurking. You really have got to spy. If he knows you're there, the whole thing'll fall apart. He'll put on a show for you – do a full day's work just to make you look foolish.'

'Yes, I suppose you're right,' Sarah agreed glumly. 'Mind

you, I don't think I could feel more foolish than I do now.' She shook her head angrily. 'Oh, I should really have challenged him with it on Friday, but, I don't know . . . he just seemed so straight and honest and charming.'

'You mean you looked into those great big brown eyes?'

'I suppose I did.'

'Fatal. But listen, this time you've really got to find out the truth.' Sarah nodded ruefully. 'Otherwise you'll never get it sorted out. What you must do is keep out of sight, pretend you've gone off to work in the morning, see how soon after you've apparently left he goes out, then, when he comes back, confront him with the fact that you know he's doing another job.'

Another rueful nod. 'Yes. As ever, Russell, you make it sound easy.'

'Don't you think you can manage?'

'I don't know. It's the sort of thing Henry would have done – though of course Henry would never have let it get to this stage . . .' Again the edge of doubt came in to her mind. *Would* Henry really have coped with the situation? She had a little flutter of panic that her image of her late husband was becoming hazy. Still, no time for that kind of fruitless introspection. 'Oh, I'll try, Russell. I'll do my best.'

He stared at her for a moment over his half-glasses, then seemed to reach a decision. 'Look, I reckon the shop could do without me for a couple of hours in the morning. Would it help if I came along?'

It was painfully tempting, but she knew she must refuse. 'Oh, that's sweet of you. But no, you already take quite enough, just listening to me maundering on. I can't let you get involved in this. It's my problem.'

'But surely it'd help if I came along . . . just for the first bit of spying . . . you know, to give you moral support.'

'Of course it'd help, Russell. It's just that I don't feel I should batten on you for –'

'You're not battening. Battening isn't in your nature, Sarah. You're one of the least battening people I know.'

She grinned.

'Look,' said Russell, 'it's a genuine offer. I wouldn't make it if I didn't mean it.'

'Well . . .'

'Come on, I'm intrigued, apart from anything else. I've heard so much about this potential cowboy, I want to witness the final shoot-out.'

'I don't think it'll be High Noon,' said Sarah gloomily. 'More like Custer's Last Stand.'

'Well, I'd still like to be part of it. Sarah, just give me a straight answer to a straight question – Would it help if I was there with you tomorrow morning?'

'Yes, Russell. Of course it would.'

'Good,' he said, picking up a copy of *Fabian Essays in Socialism* with a triumphant smile. 'That's settled then.'

Chapter 14

Unmasking the Villain

Sarah felt ridiculously surreptitious the next morning, but now she was committed to her course of espionage, there was no going back. She kept her plans from the other members of the family. In Eleanor's new mood of righteousness, there was no telling what she might do if she knew what was afoot; she was quite capable of going down and warning Terry of the plot against him.

And as for confiding in her daughter . . . well, Sarah didn't want to prompt any more accusations of suspicion and crabbiness. So when, at half-past eight, Clare, drinking coffee in the kitchen, asked why her mother hadn't started for work, Sarah fudged round the answer.

'There's no hurry,' she said. 'Russell's opening the shop a

bit later today.' Which, she congratulated herself, was not actually a lie.

'Huh,' Clare snorted. 'All right for some. I wish the building society sometimes decided to open a bit later.'

'Well, it doesn't, so perhaps you ought to be on your way.'

Clare nodded agreement, and gulped down the remains of her coffee.

'Are you sure you've had enough breakfast?' The words came out before Sarah could stop them.

Her daughter rounded on her. 'You know, Mummy, one thing I'm longing for more than any other is the day when I can leave the house without hearing any inquiries about how much breakfast I've eaten.'

Sarah was properly contrite.

'Which,' Clare continued, 'I will be able to do when I live in the flat. Assuming the flat ever exists.'

'Don't worry,' said Sarah, with a confidence she didn't quite feel. 'It's in hand.'

'Glad to hear it. Has anyone informed Terry of that?'

'He'll find out.' Sarah was unwilling to volunteer more information, and fortunately Clare didn't follow up.

'Good,' she said, on her way out of the kitchen. 'See you later, Mummy. 'Bye.'

Clare grabbed her coat and bag from the hall, and was surprised, on opening the front door, to be confronted by her mother's boss.

She greeted him with some bewilderment, but Russell reciprocated her greeting as if there was nothing unusual in his appearance on Sarah's doorstep at that hour of the morning.

'Bit of a surprise to see you here now,' Clare probed.

'Yes, isn't it?' he agreed pleasantly, but unhelpfully. He stood aside to let her pass. 'Have a good day.'

'Thank you,' she said. ''Bye.' And she set off down the path with a puzzled expression on her face.

Russell went in through the front door and called out softly to Sarah. She appeared in the hall, guiltily flushed. 'Oh, morning. Thanks for coming, Russell. You know, I feel like a criminal.'

'You shouldn't,' he reassured her. 'Right is on your side. If anything, you should feel like a law-enforcement officer, out to catch the malefactor.'

'Yes.' Again doubts assailed her. 'If he is one. I'm going to feel terrible if I find out there really is some perfectly innocent explanation for what he's doing.'

'I think we've ruled out that possibility,' said Russell grimly. 'Just you wait and see. As soon as he arrives, I bet he'll be straight off to his other job – that's if he bothers to turn up at all.'

'Ah, now, he has been very punctilious about arriving on time every other morning.'

'Yes, but he said he was going to be late today, didn't he?'

'Nine o'clock.'

'Safely after you should have left for work.'

'But he said he was buying materials,' protested Sarah weakly, still trying to think the best of everyone.

'Well, we'll see.' Then Russell added darkly, 'I wonder whose materials you'll be being charged for this time . . .?'

Sarah's face took on a helpless look. 'If he doesn't turn up, we'll look pretty silly with our stake-out, won't we?'

'Maybe. But at least we'll have positive proof of what he's up to.' Russell inspected the hall. 'Now where's going to be our best vantage point? Somewhere where we can hear – and ideally see – exactly what goes on. Is there a separate entrance to the basement?'

'There is, but it's locked. He has to come in by the front door, come through here, and go down to the basement by . . .' – she pointed – 'that door.'

'Right.' Russell looked around calculatingly. 'So if we secrete ourselves in the sitting-room, and leave the door ajar, we'll be able to see and hear everything.'

'Yes . . .' Sarah still felt rather bad about it all. 'Would you like a cup of coffee before we start?'

Russell shook his head solemnly. 'No. If Terry smells recently made coffee, he's going to get suspicious, isn't he?'

Oh dear, thought Sarah, thank goodness I never had to work in the French Resistance or anything like that. I'd have been utterly hopeless at it.

Anyone who fancies feeling truly stupid should try hiding in their own sitting-room, waiting to spy on a builder who might or might not be ripping them off. It certainly worked for Sarah. As the minutes ticked by towards nine o'clock, she felt more and more of a lemon. And, somehow, the gravity with which Russell was treating the situation only made things worse. She had an inappropriate urge to giggle.

Terry quickly removed any doubts as to whether he was going to turn up or not. On the dot of nine o'clock, footsteps approached the front door and keys rattled in the lock.

'Can't fault him for time-keeping,' Sarah hissed in Russell's ear.

'Depends who's paying for the time, though,' came the dampening response.

Through the thin line between the hinges of the door, they saw Terry come in and close the front door. He was carrying two large pots of paint and some bulging brown paper bags, so he had at least been telling the truth about buying materials. But who were those materials for? And would they be used in the service of the person on whose bill they appeared?

He was again whistling cheerily and, as ever, the sight of him, so friendly and ingenuous-looking, brought Sarah a new surge of guilt for all the evil thoughts she had been entertaining.

The builder wiped his feet religiously on the doormat, crossed straight to the door to the basement, and went through out of sight of his unknown investigators.

Sarah felt relieved. She really *did* want her suspicions to prove unfounded. With a look almost of triumph at Russell, she said, 'Straight down to work. Perhaps I have been maligning him.'

'Depends how long he stays down there,' Russell observed gloomily.

But Sarah's new optimism was not to be so easily dented. 'He'll probably be down there all day. A full, conscientious eight hours. Goodness, I really would be relieved if that happened. These suspicions are tearing me apart.'

Russell, however, still had no reassurance to offer. 'If it takes him eight hours a day to do as little as you say he's doing, then he's either utterly dishonest or utterly incompetent. Either way you want to be shot of him.'

Sarah wanted to continue her embattled defence of Terry, but was stopped by the sound of footsteps coming up from the basement. Russell shook his head ruefully.

'Might just be making a cup of coffee,' Sarah mouthed with fading hope, but Russell's head shook even more firmly.

The watchers saw Terry emerge from the basement door and make for the kitchen. This was encouraging, as it supported Sarah's 'cup of coffee' theory. But just as he was about to enter the kitchen, something totally unexpected happened. A voice from the stairs called his name, and, reluctantly, Terry turned towards the sound.

The voice was one that Sarah would have recognized through seventeen layers of concrete, and as she listened to the ensuing conversation, understanding came quickly. Understanding was instantly followed by fury.

'Good morning,' said the voice, in its well-modulated, middle-class tones.

'Good morning,' the builder replied, and then said hastily, 'I was only going to make a cup of coffee. I haven't really got time to –'

'Oh, it's nothing much,' the invisible Eleanor's voice said silkily. 'I was wondering if you could just come up and have a little look at this place where I want the work-surface to be.'

Terry looked apologetic. 'I really think I ought to be getting on downstairs. I mean, I'm pretty much behind as it is and what with –'

'It'll only take a minute,' Eleanor breezed.

'That's what you said about the wallpapering. And putting up the kitchen units.'

Sarah's eyes bulged, as the full enormity of what had been going on struck her. All kinds of little details fell into place. She hadn't really noticed over the weekend how Eleanor had kept her out of the upstairs flat, but of course it had been carefully planned. All those specious excuses about burning milk-pans. The piously shocked refusal to spy on Terry herself. It was Eleanor at her most devious.

Sarah rose to go and confront her mother, but felt Russell's restraining hand on her arm. She looked at him, grimacing her anger and intentions, but he mimed back, indicating Terry.

Yes, of course. Any challenge to Eleanor at that moment would expose the fact that they were spying on the builder, leaving no doubt about the suspicions Sarah had been harbouring. It would be better to wait and take her mother to task later. That way Terry need never know. And, since it now seemed that, far from being the villain of the piece, he was as much a victim as Sarah, it was better to keep him in the dark.

So she resigned herself to hearing out the rest of the conversation between the honest builder and her perfidious mother.

Eleanor's voice was at its most charming. 'Oh, please, Terry. As a favour.'

'Well . . .' The builder hesitated. 'Look, are you sure your daughter doesn't mind me doing all this?'

'No, she'll be delighted.' Sarah clenched her fists as she heard this. 'She'll love to see my little kitchen-diner properly brightened up.'

'Then why don't you want me to tell her about it?' asked Terry, reasonably enough.

'Because I want her to see the full effect when it's finished. Sarah just loves surprises.'

The lover of surprises in question had to gag herself with her fist to stop any sound coming out after this brazen assertion.

Terry weakened and moved hesitantly towards the foot of the stairs. 'If you're sure . . .'

Eleanor's voice faded away as she led him up to her flat again. 'As I say, it's just this work-surface. I only want you to take a look at it . . .'

Terry sighed, and his voice too faded as he followed her. 'All right. I'll just take a quick look, but . . .'

Russell and Sarah looked at each other. Behind the sympathy in his eye, there was a twinkle of humour as he said, 'Well.'

Sarah was in no mood to see the funny side. 'As you say, well,' she hissed.

'It seems as if we have found the other job that Terry keeps going off to.'

'Yes,' she agreed venomously. 'Love surprises, do I? Well, I hope my bloody mother loves them too – because she's certainly got one coming to her!'

The confrontation had to wait until the end of the day, when Terry, innocent of the calumnies heaped upon his head, had left after his conscientious eight hours in the house (though not in the part of the house where he was supposed to have done them).

Sarah lured her unsuspecting mother down to the sitting-room with a polite offer of sherry and, as soon as they were both armed with drinks, made it clear that she knew everything.

Eleanor could never be accused of lacking coolness. Even through her current fury, Sarah was forced to admit that, when, with a little, bewildered smile, her mother said, 'But, Sarah dear, it never occurred to me that you might mind.'

'You are an old humbug – not to say a liar.'

Eleanor looked pained. 'I don't think it's very polite to speak to your mother in that way, Sarah.'

This was a typical Eleanor ploy, going on to the attack when the appropriate reaction should be apology. But Sarah wasn't going to have her momentum slowed. 'Mother, don't you dare start getting on your high horse just because you haven't got a leg to stand on.'

'You're mixing your metaphors, dear,' Eleanor observed infuriatingly.

'And don't try to distract me from the subject! You deliberately took advantage of that young man's goodwill.'

'Nonsense.' Eleanor dismissed the accusation with a shrug. 'He just happened to be in the house, and I just happened to ask his advice on a matter of decoration, and then I just suggested that he might have the odd moment to help out an old pensioner, and he's such an obliging young man . . .'

'Yes, he is,' Sarah agreed bitterly. 'One of nature's gentlemen. One of those very rare people who is genuinely altruistic, who really is willing to do someone a favour without any hope of return.' She rounded on her mother. 'As a result of your little games, do you know the kind of suspicions of him I was harbouring? Do you realize I almost ended up accusing him of fraud? At one stage I even contemplated bringing the police in!'

'I cannot help it,' her mother had the nerve to say, 'if you have a suspicious nature.'

'No,' Sarah snapped back, 'but you can help it if you have a deceitful one!'

At this, frailty was instantly switched on. 'That's not a very kind thing to say to an old lady, dear.'

'Maybe not, but it's true. You planned this whole thing. You knew exactly what you were doing at every turn. You kept me out of your flat deliberately, so that I wouldn't see what was going on. All you wanted was to get your kitchen-diner decorated.'

'Well, I got it,' Eleanor announced complacently. 'Didn't I, dear?'

'Yes. At my expense!'

This idea was dismissed with an airy wave of the hand. 'Oh, it hardly cost a thing. Just the odd scrap of wallpaper, a few bits of wood . . . And it's not as if Terry wasn't here, anyway.'

'Yes, but *I* was paying for him being here.'

'Oh, I never thought of that aspect of it.'

'Liar!' said Sarah.

This time Eleanor at least had the grace not to contest the accusation. Instead, with irritating smugness, she observed, 'Still, it does look nice. Terry's done a very good job on it. You must come and have a look, dear. You'll be very impressed. And, at least,' she added triumphantly, 'I did get it done.'

Sarah agreed. 'Oh yes, you got it done. But you got it done by deceit!'

Her mother raised a correcting finger. 'No, dear.'

'No?'

'No.' And Eleanor produced one of those ingenious perversions of logic, with which her daughter had been regularly confronted ever since she could remember. 'You see, deceit is being dishonest to people you don't know well.'

'And what's being dishonest to those nearest and dearest to you?' asked Sarah, resigned to getting a reply whose total independence of the traditional rules of reasoning would make it unanswerable.

She was not disappointed.

'That, Sarah,' her mother explained with a helpful smile, 'is just part of the give-and-take of family life.'

Chapter 15

Positive Thinking

Once Terry had got his 'other job' out of the way, he progressed quickly on the basement conversion, and by mid-November, Clare had a flat to move into. He had done an excellent job and presented a final bill which (if one excluded the cost of the work done on Eleanor's flat) came in well under his original estimate. Sarah thanked him enormously, tipped him generously, and experienced terrible cold shivers every time she contemplated what might have happened if she'd ever voiced her suspicions of this saint among builders.

Clare was over the moon about her flat. It was hers, it gave her the privacy she required, and yet there was the reassuring knowledge that an apron-string was not far away to be reached for. Clare firmly intended never to reach for it, but its presence remained comforting.

Almost instantly the relationship between Sarah and her daughter improved. Much of the friction between them had been caused by simple proximity. Now Clare had her own entrance, could conduct her own life, and invite her own friends round without reference to anyone.

She could also invite her mother and grandmother round, and, in doing so, she followed that basic rule of family planning – inviting them separately. This worked very well. Rather than bumping into each other all the time, the three now had social events to look forward to. Clare would issue an invitation to Sarah or Eleanor for tea, supper or whatever, and it would become an occasion, not just the grudging encounter of people brought together by geographical contiguity, but a treat for which some effort should be made.

It was still rare for a day to go past without each of the three women seeing the other two, however briefly, but a definite advance had been made in Clare's relationships with her mother and grandmother.

Clare's example did not, unfortunately, appear to change Eleanor's habits and put her encounters with Sarah on an 'invitation only' basis. She still wandered in and out of her daughter's part of the house at will, but then, Sarah reflected, you can't have everything.

The success of her flat conversion idea, and of her choice of builder (on which she could now, in retrospect, safely congratulate herself), together with the knowledge that these decisions had been her own, unaided work, gave Sarah another surge of confidence. This was a rare sensation in the years since Henry's death; at first she had difficulty in recognizing the unfamiliar feeling. And, when she had identified it, she treated it with some circumspection, aware of its fragility and unwilling to frighten it away.

But it was an encouraging sign. Once again a little chink of light showed, the possibility that she could develop a life of her own. It would never be the same as it had been with Henry, but the future might still hold excitements for her.

Moments after the confidence had arrived, its tedious companion, guilt, limped up to join it. Just as when she had been flattered by Nick's attentions, or when she had felt elated on the journey to see Janie, such positive thinking brought with it the fear of betraying Henry's memory.

But this time she coped with the reaction better. She recognized it as something she would always carry with her, but did not let it drag down her mood quite as much as it had done in the past. This had to be the way forward, she felt sure. The pangs would never go away completely, but each time they came, it would be perhaps with a reduced power. Anguish would be diluted to sadness, and then sadness might, in time, melt into wistfulness.

She was making positive progress. Only a few months before, even the thought of tidying the basement had felt like a betrayal of mutual plans she and Henry had made for it; and yet now it had actually been turned into a flat. Yes, she was getting there.

This new confidence was so strong that she even dared to raise the subject of Christmas. It was at a Sunday lunch a couple of weeks after Clare had moved in downstairs, one of those, now rarer, occasions when all three women were together.

They had had a good, traditional roast and trimmings, had put paid to one bottle of Beaujolais and were making healthy inroads into a second as they ate their apple crumble. The atmosphere between them was relaxed, even mellow, so Sarah seized the bull by the horns and announced, 'We ought to decide what we're going to do about Christmas.'

This prompted a groan from Clare and a quizzical look from Eleanor. Sarah pressed on, 'Well, we really should. It's not much more than a month away, and we must start thinking about what we're going to do . . .'

The sentence trickled away. She didn't spell out how desperately she needed a Christmas without comparisons, a Christmas that wasn't a carbon copy of the last two Christmases, occasions which she had only been made increasingly – and painfully – aware of Henry's absence. Surely the other two knew what she had been through. She didn't have to spell it out for them.

Eleanor's reaction suggested that, for her at least, a bit of spelling-out might be necessary. 'Well,' she said, 'it's obvious, isn't it?'

'Is it?' asked Sarah.

'It's Christmas, after all,' Eleanor explained patiently. 'We'll do what we always do.'

'Yes.'

Sarah sounded uncertain, and was relieved when Clare weighed in on her side, announcing, 'But I don't think what we always do works.'

Good old Clare. Establish the idea of change, then press home the advantage.

'What do you mean?' asked Eleanor, affronted.

'I mean I don't enjoy it.'

Thank God someone's said the words out loud, thought Sarah. I felt sure I wasn't the only one.

Eleanor turned a severe eye on her granddaughter. 'Clare, Christmas is a family time. That means you spend it with your family. Whether you enjoy it or not is neither here nor there.'

Her mother's words did rather close the conversation, but Sarah was not too cast down. The subject had been broached, that was the main thing. And Clare had even voiced the heresy that it was possible not to enjoy Christmas. It was a starting-point. They would come back to the problem again. Sarah was determined that this year they would break with the tradition of a Christmas when they all pretended that Henry was still there.

So her new confidence was not too badly dented. In fact, she still felt positive and capable.

And, to demonstrate to herself just how positive and capable she felt, that evening she rang up Clifford and Gwen Davies. They were the couple, long on her social conscience, to whom she owed a dinner from over two years before.

The new positive, capable Sarah France therefore invited them to dinner for the following Friday week. And Gwen Davies, who had answered the phone in her little wispy Welsh voice, said yes, they were free, they'd love to come.

The acceptance threw Sarah into a momentary panic, so as soon as she put the phone down, she rang Russell and invited him, too. He sounded a little surprised, but accepted.

Good, she thought, I'll have at least one friendly face at my dinner party.

And, at the same moment, the new positive, capable Sarah made a decision about someone else whom she *wouldn't* be having at her dinner party.

Eleanor was a great reader. That is to say, she was often to be seen with a book in her hand. But a book, for her, was, like everything else in her life, a potential source of power. She could refer to its contents to draw disparaging comparisons, she could bury her head in it to exclude unwelcome conversations, or she could use it as yet another excuse to muscle in on her daughter's privacy.

'Hope you don't mind, dear,' the typical ploy would run, as she appeared in Sarah's kitchen or sitting-room, 'I've been on my own all day, so I thought I'd just slip down and sit with you and read. You don't have to make conversation, dear. Carry on with what you're doing. Don't take any notice of me. Just pretend I'm not here.'

Sarah, who had devoted forty-two years of hard graft to trying to pretend her mother wasn't there, now knew the impossibility of the task, and so would resign herself to an evening of constant interruptions, until even the pretence of reading was abandoned, as Eleanor settled in for a good gossip.

What annoyed her daughter even more was that, for invasions of this sort, Eleanor produced a complete alternative library. Just as she would switch over from the television situation comedies she enjoyed to earnest documentaries when someone appeared in the room, so she abandoned her habitual diet of Jackie Collins or Judith Krantz and, for excursions into Sarah's part of the house, would appear clutching a worthy tome by Doris Lessing or A. S. Byatt.

Not that a lot of reading got done on these occasions. The book was merely the pretext, the thin end of yet another wedge being driven into Sarah's independence.

The latest of this series of reading incursions took place on the Tuesday after the Christmas discussion. And it was made doubly annoying because Sarah was trying to read, too. That is to say, she was in the kitchen, going through recipe books, searching out the right menu for the following Friday night. It was a long time since she had done this kind of entertaining and she was disproportionately anxious about getting things right.

Eleanor sat demurely beside her at the kitchen table in the unlikely company of Nadine Gordimer and, give her her due, she did turn over a dutiful five pages before making it overtly apparent that she was much more interested in her daughter's reading matter than her own.

'Mother,' Sarah protested finally, 'I do wish you'd stop

looking over my shoulder. There is nothing more distracting than having someone trying to read what you're reading.'

'I know, Sarah dear,' Eleanor agreed.

'If you know, why do you do it?'

'Just showing an interest.'

'Well, how about showing an interest in your own book instead?'

'Yes, dear. Of course, dear.' Another two pages of Nadine Gordimer were punctiliously flicked over before Eleanor spoke again. 'Oh, I wouldn't give them that, Sarah.'

'What?'

Eleanor pointed to the page at which the recipe book was open. 'Those potatoes in garlic mayonnaise. I mean, garlic is a very strong taste and you don't want your dinner guests going home reeking of it, do you?'

Sarah slammed her book shut. 'Mother, will you mind your own bloody business!'

'There is no need to swear, Sarah.' Eleanor sniffed. 'But you've made your point. I will be as quiet as a mouse. Not a sound will you hear from me.' She settled back into Nadine Gordimer, but this time only one page was turned before she said, 'I don't see why you're making such a fuss about this dinner party.'

'Mother . . .!' Sarah hissed.

'It's not as if you haven't given dinner parties before.'

'I haven't given many since Henry died.'

'I don't see what difference that makes.' Now all pretence had gone. Nadine Gordimer lay firmly closed on the kitchen table.

'It makes a huge difference,' said Sarah, drawn unwillingly into argument. 'I mean, just having to make all the preparations on my own. Without Henry.'

'He never helped you prepare dinner parties.'

'No, but at least he was there.'

'Not all the time. He kept being called out on emergencies.'

This was actually true, but Sarah tried to explain how important the possibility of her husband's presence had been.

Eleanor gave another sniff. 'I still don't see what difference it makes.'

Sarah tried reason. You could never be sure, it *might* work. 'Oh, come on, Mother, you must have felt the same when Daddy died. The difficulty of entertaining on your own.'

'Not really.' Too late, Sarah realized that she had given the wrong prompt and shoved her mother into We Were So Poor Mode. 'But then of course we didn't ever entertain in the same lavish way that you do. The money just wasn't around when we were first married. We had to scrimp and save to keep you fed and clothed. There wasn't a lot left to spend on garlic mayonnaise for our friends. I think what you forget, Sarah, is that –'

'All right, Mother, all right. I don't want the complete history of the Depression. Yes,' she parroted, 'I have been very privileged and I am duly appreciative of my good fortune. *But* the fact remains that I still feel odd setting up a dinner party on my own.'

'You miss the calming presence of someone with a bit of confidence, a bit of *savoir-faire*, to help you?' asked Eleanor sympathetically.

'Exactly. I'm glad you've got the point at last.'

Eleanor's next words suggested that she hadn't got the point at all. 'Don't worry, dear. I'll help you.'

'What? No. No, I don't think that's a good idea.'

'It's no trouble. I'm quite prepared to put myself out for you.'

'I dare say, but I'm not quite sure that I –'

'But, Sarah, don't be silly.' Eleanor shook her head at her

daughter's perverseness. 'If I'm going to be at this dinner party, then I might just as well help you prepare it.'

Oh dear. No, she hadn't got the point at all, had she? Sarah had hoped that Clare's new 'by invitation only' policy might have brought home to Eleanor the significance of the fact that no invitation for the following Friday had been issued to her. But no, it wasn't going to be as easy as that.

For a moment, Sarah contented herself with saying, 'Ah.'

'What do you mean – ah?'

Time to tread warily. 'I mean, Mother, that I hadn't actually planned on your being at this dinner party.'

'Oh?' Eleanor could sometimes be amazingly obtuse. 'Why? I'm free that evening.'

'But I thought you played bridge with Winifred every Friday.'

'Yes, normally I do,' Eleanor agreed. 'But, because this is a special occasion, I put Winifred off. She fully understood.'

'Yes.' No way round it. Have to be brutal. Frontal attack. Deep breath. Here we go. 'What I'm actually saying, Mother, is that I was not intending you to be at this dinner party.'

Eleanor had a wide repertoire of reactions to things she didn't want to hear. Recently she had been starting to favour the most literal of them. 'I'm sorry, Sarah? What did you say? As you know, I'm getting rather deaf.'

Sarah enunciated her reply very clearly. The elocution mistress, to whom her mother had insisted she went, would have been proud of her pupil. 'I said, Mother, that you are not invited for next Friday.'

Deafness having failed to divert the unwelcome news, Eleanor tried incomprehension. 'I don't understand.'

'I can't put it any plainer than that. Look,' Sarah explained, 'I am setting up a dinner party, and I want it to be a nice, civilized, adult occasion. Do you understand now?'

The dropping of the penny could be delayed no longer.

Eleanor drew in a deep breath of disapproval. 'Oh yes. Fully. The way you see it, I am not nice . . .'

'I didn't say –'

'I am uncivilized . . .'

'Mother . . .'

'And I am in my second childhood.'

'I didn't mean that,' said Sarah, thinking, Couldn't you just, for once in your life, *under*react to something? 'All I meant, Mother, was that Clifford and Gwen are not people I know very well, and I want, I suppose, to impress them – without being constantly brought down by you.'

As an attempt at tact, this was no more successful than her previous effort. Eleanor bridled. 'Brought down – by your own mother? Are you suggesting that I am not a suitable parent for you?'

'No. I'm just saying that you still treat me as if I were a bloody teenager!'

'There's no need to swear,' said Eleanor instinctively, proving her daughter's point.

'See what I mean? I know what you're like. Just when I'm doing my best to be suave and sophisticated, you'll come in and undermine me with some anecdote of how I used to behave when I was a child.'

'I won't.'

'Of course you will. All mothers do. It's one of their functions.'

'Not one of *my* functions. I've never done anything like that. I think you're being most insensitive.' Then, once again proving Sarah's point, Eleanor slipped into reminiscence. 'You've always had this streak in you, you know, Sarah. I remember, when you were at school, you didn't want me to come to Speech Day one year because you were afraid I'd tell Miss Thorp you had a crush on her.'

Sarah nodded vigorously. 'And I was right – you did tell her!'

Her mother smiled at the recollection. 'She was very amused.'

'Yes, but I wasn't!' With an effort, Sarah restrained her anger and tried a gentler, more conciliatory approach. 'Look, I'm sorry, Mother. I know it sounds as if I'm being rotten, but I really think I will be able to cope with this dinner party better without you. Please understand. It's nothing personal.'

'No. No, of course not. Nothing personal.' Eleanor paused, gathering her energy to make the transition into Supermartyr Mode. 'I'm only your mother, after all, so one wouldn't really expect there to be anything personal, would one?'

Sarah tried to deflect her with a remonstrating 'Mother . . .', but Eleanor was magnificently under way, and nothing short of an Exocet would stop her.

'Don't worry about me, Sarah,' she said, in a voice of noble suffering. 'I'll be fine. There's always the television, after all. A lot of elderly people find the television's a great comfort . . . when their family drifts away.'

And, picking up her Nadine Gordimer, she moved out of the kitchen towards the next Station of the Cross.

Chapter 16

Not Doing Anything Right

Russell looked up mildly from his study of the 1646 first edition of *Pseudodoxia Epidemica*. The books really were being dusted with unaccustomed vigour. And they were being slammed rather than placed on to the shelves.

He closed Sir Thomas Browne's inquiry into vulgar errors and reached round for a book from the 'Robustly Anti-Catholic Literature' shelf behind him. He held it out towards Sarah.

'Here, this may help. Make you realize that your mother's not the only one.'

Sarah turned tetchily from her dusting. 'What is it?' But when she saw what he was proffering, she smiled and said, 'Very good, Russell, very good.'

The book was Volume III of the Cattley and Townsend edition of Foxe's *Book of Martyrs*.

'Only the one,' Russell observed sadly. 'All eight volumes might actually be worth a few bob.'

'Well,' said Sarah, 'if they ever come to revise it, my mother should get a whole chapter to herself. Honestly, you'd think I'd tried to murder her or something. She creeps round the house, with an expression of pained reproach etched on her forehead, and pretends that she's deaf.' Sarah dropped into her long-practised – and uncannily accurate – impression of Eleanor. '"Not that it matters about an elderly person being deaf – it only matters for people who get talked to a lot." All this is said in a little, little voice. "It's all right, Sarah. There's no need to worry about me, Sarah."' A sigh of exasperation. 'I think that's the most disturbing thing a mother can ever say – "There's no need to worry about me." It instantly throws her children into paroxysms of anxiety.'

'Which is, of course, what it's meant to do.'

'Oh yes, I know that, Russell. I should think my bloody mother'll see to it that her dying words are "There's no need to worry about me." Leaving me the rest of my life to try and work out what I should have been worrying about.'

Russell chuckled. 'And all this, the full Greek tragedy, because you don't want her at your dinner party?'

'Yes.'

'Hmm. Makes me feel almost guilty for being on the magic list of people who *are* invited.' There was something strange in Russell's intonation, the same note that had been in his voice when Sarah had rung up and issued the invitation. She could not quite identify what it was.

'Don't feel guilty,' she said. 'You'll earn every last after-dinner mint.'

Russell nodded pensively. 'These Clifford and Gwen people are a bit daunting, are they?'

'Quite honestly, I can't remember them that well,' she confessed. 'They invited us to dinner just before Henry died, and for the last two years I've been plucking up courage to ask them back. From what I recall, Gwen's all right. When she's allowed to get a word out. Clifford's very Welsh, can be a bit overpowering. Rather, er, forthright, in his opinions.'

'How did you meet them?'

'Henry used to come across Clifford in the course of work. He's in hospital administration. Henry managed him quite well, used to keep sending him up all the time. Not that Clifford realized he was being sent up.' A sudden draught of doubt chilled her. 'I'm not sure that I'll be able to manage that.'

'I'll be there,' said Russell. But behind the reassurance in his voice, there was that other quality of restraint Sarah could still not quite identify.

'Bless you, Russell. I can't thank you enough for helping me out.'

'One thing I wanted to ask . . .' he began slowly. 'Am I gay?'

She chuckled. 'What do you mean? I thought that was one of the major discoveries of your life.'

He smiled, but it was still a restrained smile. 'Yes, of course. But I meant – am I gay for the purposes of your dinner party?'

'Oh, I see.'

'I mean, since you didn't invite Bob, do I presume that I'm going to be there masquerading as your latest romantic interest?'

'Good heavens, no.' As she said it, Sarah understood. She now knew exactly why Russell had sounded strange when accepting her invitation, and why he was behaving oddly that morning. She had made a major social gaffe. She spent so much time with Russell, he was such a good friend, that she was sometimes in danger of forgetting his gayness. And now she had offended him deeply by inviting him out without his boyfriend.

She tried to mend the broken fence. 'I'm sorry. I feel awful now. I should have invited Bob, shouldn't I?'

But she wasn't going to be let off the hook that easily. 'He'll be all right,' said Russell. 'He could take your mother out for the evening. They could sit over a bottle of vitriol and bitch about you.'

'Look, I do apologize. I just wasn't thinking. Is he terribly upset?'

'No, he's all right. Don't worry about it.' But the airiness of the reply still did not contain complete forgiveness.

Sarah continued trying to make things better. 'You must both come round. Really. I mean, on a more . . . suitable occasion.'

Russell looked her straight in the eye. 'From which I gather that one of Clifford's "forthright" opinions is a disapproval of homosexuals.'

She hadn't thought of it, but, now Russell mentioned the idea, she had a horrible feeling he might be right. God, why had she ever been so stupid as to think of giving a dinner party?

She tried to pass the moment off with a light touch. 'I wouldn't say that, Russell, no. It's just that Clifford and Gwen are terribly boring and, when you and Bob come round, I'd like it to be a really fun evening.'

'Though you don't mind me on my own being bored to tears?' he asked implacably.

Sarah sighed. 'I can't say anything right at the moment.'

Russell allowed her a small grin. 'Sarah, I am sending you up.'

'Are you really?' she asked, uncertain.

'Of course.' He was nearly telling the truth, but not quite. She had offended him through sheer carelessness, and it would take a long time for the memory of the offence to fade away completely.

'I wish I'd never contemplated this dinner party. Every arrangement I make for it seems to upset someone.'

'I'm not upset. Really.' Russell's assertion might have convinced someone who didn't know him as well as Sarah did. 'What about Clare, though? Have you upset her yet?'

Sarah scrabbled greedily for this one, tiny crumb of comfort. 'Not about this, no. I think for once I have actually done something that doesn't upset my daughter. In fact, since she's been in the flat and got a bit of freedom, the occasions for my upsetting Clare have diminished significantly. No,' Sarah continued, a little, faltering confidence creeping back into her, 'so long as she isn't expected to come to it, I think I can confidently say that nothing about this dinner party will upset Clare.'

'Oh, Mummy!' said Clare that evening, instantly disproving the assertion that Sarah had made to Russell. 'I think that's utterly inconsiderate – setting up a dinner party for next Friday. I told you weeks and weeks ago that I was going to have my flat-warming then.'

'But –'

'Didn't I?'

'Yes, yes,' Sarah was forced to admit, 'you did. I'm sorry, Clare, but you told me so many weeks and weeks ago that it completely slipped my mind and, when Clifford and Gwen said they were free for next Friday, I just sort of leapt at the date and –'

'Mummy, if you can't organize your own social diary, that's hardly my fault, is it?'

'No, no. Fair enough.' There was no profit in arguing. It

was black and white. Clare was in the right, and Sarah was in the wrong. She looked round her kitchen and tried to remind herself that there had been a time in the past when she had been capable of having good ideas. The flat. Yes, Clare's flat. That had been a good idea. That had worked.

But this comforting thought was quickly dashed away when she realized a disturbing consequence of having forgotten Clare's party. 'Oh dear. And another nice, neat idea goes out of the window.'

'What nice, neat idea?' asked Clare, suspicious on principle of her mother's nice, neat ideas.

'I just thought it would be wonderfully convenient if you happened to be free to take your grandmother out to the cinema on that Friday evening.'

'Well, I won't be free, will I?'

'No, I can see that. If you've actually invited everyone . . .'

'I haven't invited anyone,' said Clare.

A chink of hope. 'Oh, then perhaps you could change the date and you could –'

'I haven't *invited* anyone,' Clare explained patiently, 'but they're all coming.'

'Oh.' Sarah frowned in puzzlement. 'Clare, I'm sorry to sound obtuse, but if you haven't invited anyone, what makes you think anyone's going to turn up?'

Clare sighed, pitying such ignorance. 'Mummy, in my crowd we don't invite people to parties.'

'No?'

'No, that's terribly middle-aged.'

Go on, rub it in, thought Sarah. I didn't think anything could make me feel more middle-aged today, but maybe you can find a little something.

'Then what will make them come to the party?' she asked wearily. 'Telepathy?'

'No. We just let them know that the party's likely to happen.'

'But you don't invite them.'

'No.'

Sarah nodded, pretending that this made sense.

'Anyway,' Clare concluded, 'I can't change it now. It's all set up.'

'You mean everyone knows it's likely to happen?'

'Exactly,' Clare replied, glad that her mother had at last got the point.

'Including dear Gary with the pink hair and the earrings?'

'Mummy, I know you don't approve of –'

Sarah raised a conciliatory hand. 'I didn't say a word.'

'Anyway, you won't have to see him. In fact,' said Clare, thinking about it, 'if you come near my flat that evening, I'll murder you.'

'Wild horses wouldn't drag me there,' Sarah assured her.

'It won't be your scene.'

'That I believe.' Then she thought of the kind of scene it might be. 'Um, Clare, I'm really sorry about this clash of dates, but since it's happened, and since your living-room's directly below my dining-room, could I just mention music? I'd really appreciate it if –'

'That's a thought, yes,' said Clare, getting in first. 'Mummy, if you maintain your habit of having tasteful background music going through your dinner party, could you keep the volume down? My friends won't want Vivaldi pounding through the floorboards at them all evening.'

Touché, thought Sarah. One thing she could never fault her daughter for was the speed of her reactions. 'Actually, Clare, I was going to say the same to you. If you're planning to play all your favourite cassettes at –'

'Modern music,' Clare announced, 'is produced specifically with a view to being played at high volume.'

'OK, I'll take your word for that, but I'm just asking you

to moderate it. My friends won't want the Top Twenty pounding through –'

Clare looked at her pityingly and said, with icy dignity, 'Mummy, I don't give that sort of party.'

'Oh. I'm sorry. I just wanted to be sure that –'

The kitchen door opened. Eleanor drifted in, head held high. St Catherine on the way to the Wheel.

'Hello, Mother.'

'Hello, Sarah dear. Clare.' The voice was calm, ethereal, saintly. She was still very firmly in Supermartyr Mode.

'Morning, Granny.'

'How are you this morning?' asked Sarah briskly, determined not to play along with the act.

'Oh, fine. Fine.' Eleanor gave a little, noble smile. 'Don't you worry about me, dear.'

'No, I won't,' said Sarah.

'I just came to see that you were all right.'

'All right?' Sarah echoed, thrown by this sudden solicitude.

'Yes,' said Eleanor. 'Well, I read this piece in the local paper about a widow who died in her flat, and it was three weeks before anyone took the trouble to find the body.'

Don't rise, don't rise, Sarah commanded herself. Golden rule of all dealings with Mother – don't rise.

'So you're checking that I'm still alive?' she asked sardonically.

'Yes, dear.'

'Thank you.' Sarah spread her arms wide to demonstrate her continued survival. 'Well, as you see . . .'

'Oh yes, yes . . .' Eleanor moved on to her real reason for raising the subject. In a frail voice, she continued, 'Actually, of course, that sort of thing is much more likely to happen to an elderly person. The young are surrounded by love and affection, but when you're old very few people have the time to take an interest.'

Sarah's patience was wearing thin. 'Mother . . .'

Eleanor looked at her innocently. 'Sorry, dear? You know I'm a little deaf.'

'Nothing.' Sarah wasn't going to get involved in the deafness routine.

Tacitly recognizing this, Eleanor moved on to another favourite ploy. 'You know, Sarah,' she said in a voice of infinite understanding, 'I often think it might be simpler if I were to move into a home. You know, like The Sycamores, where Vera Poling is. So much less trouble for everyone.'

'Mother,' said Sarah through tight lips, 'you live in a home.'

Eleanor shook her head sadly. 'Oh, no. No, I wouldn't say that. I live in a house. I live in a small flat in a large house, where, by coincidence, my daughter also lives.'

'And your granddaughter,' Clare reminded her.

'Yes.' Eleanor, seeing an opportunity to divide and rule, favoured Clare with a smile of great sweetness. 'My granddaughter, who, I must say, is a source of great comfort to me.'

'Thank you,' said Clare brightly.

'Thank you,' said Sarah, her lips stretched to tearing point.

Eleanor, satisfied with the effect she had achieved, turned towards the door. 'Well, I mustn't keep you, Sarah. I know you've got lots to do. Just wanted to see that you're all right.'

'Are you going out?'

'Oh yes.'

'Where?'

Now it was Sarah's turn to receive the benison of a smile. 'How nice of you to ask.' Eleanor pondered for a moment. 'Well, I'm not sure, dear. I might go into the park. I could sit on a bench for a while. Or if it rains, I dare say I could find a nice cosy bus shelter.'

'Mother!' Sarah hissed, fury now threatening her vow not to rise to the bait.

'I'll be all right,' Eleanor insisted bravely, as she opened the door. 'Don't you worry about me.'

When her mother had gone, Sarah slumped forward over the table. 'Oh, my God! She drives me mad when she behaves like that.'

But there was no comfort coming from Clare. 'Does she? I thought she was being rather sweet . . . considering the way you're treating her.'

'Thank you, Clare,' said Sarah bitterly. 'When I next need support, I'll know who to come to, won't I?'

She felt utterly isolated and miserable. The confidence which had set up the dinner party had now evaporated completely. No, she wasn't the sort of person who could entertain with insouciant brilliance. She was just a drab little, sad little, widow, who was never going to recover from her husband's death.

What a mess. What an unholy, awful mess.

Still, there was no way she could get out of it. She had set up this bloody dinner party, and she was going to have to go through with it.

Chapter 17

Last-minute Preparations

Having Russell there was a help, of course it was. But at the same time his presence flustered Sarah. The hours before a dinner party are tense ones for the hostess, as she calculates a series of complicated timings for the various components of the meal and goes through flurries of panic about things she may have forgotten. It is a time when the kitchen is a sacred kingdom, over which there can only be one ruler.

And, although Russell meant well, his attention to details seemed to Sarah fussy and obtrusive. She knew she was being unfair. She knew she would have reacted the same to anyone else invading her kitchen at such a time. Even Henry would have seemed a nuisance.

But of course Henry wouldn't have been there. Either he would have ensured he only got home a few minutes before the guests arrived or, if he was in the house, he would have made himself scarce. He would have known the kind of state Sarah would have been in and kept an appropriate distance. And, if he did, by mistake, infringe her territorial rights, she would have had no compunction about shouting at him.

But she couldn't do that with Russell. He was, after all, doing her a favour by coming at all. And she'd already offended him by not inviting Bob. No, she must curb her irritation with his double-checking of everything, ignore the unexpected pernicketiness which his character displayed in a domestic setting. Just be properly grateful that he was there.

With some relief, Sarah sent him off to check the table settings, napkins and glasses in the dining-room. She also asked him to have a look at the wine and the drinks cupboard while there was still time for a last-minute mercy dash to the off-licence. That should take him a few minutes and give her time to perform a task which she had been dreading.

After consulting what seemed like every recipe book in print, she had homed in, for a sweet, on Charlotte Malakoff aux Fraises. It was something she had cooked many times before (though not for a few years) and it had always been much appreciated. But the pivotal moment, occasional past disasters had told her, was removing the refrigerated almond cream and sponge-finger delicacy from its mould. If it did break, she could always dish it out into individual serving bowls, but it looked so much better if it came out in one and could be served at the table. Anyway, doing it right was a challenge to her professional pride as a hostess.

She took the mould out of the fridge and removed the weight, plate and greaseproof paper from the top. Then, as instructed by the best cookery books, she ran a knife round the inside of the mould and placed a chilled serving dish over it. With a silent prayer, she took plate and mould in both hands and turned them upside down.

It was at this moment that she heard Russell come into the kitchen saying, 'Corkscrew? Corkscrew?'

'Corkscrew, yes. Um . . .' she said, wishing he would go away. She wanted to check the success or ruin of her Charlotte Malakoff's shape in private.

'What's that?' asked Russell curiously.

'Oh, er, sweet.'

'What is it? Are you going to lift the mould off?'

'Yes, yes, of course. But not quite yet. You'll have to wait and see.' She kept her fingers firmly on top of the mould.

'All right,' said Russell, slightly bewildered. 'What about a corkscrew, though?'

'Yes, corkscrew.' Suddenly Sarah remembered. 'Oh, my God, corkscrew!'

'You haven't got one,' Russell concluded.

'Well, yes, I have, but it's complicated. You see, yesterday evening I went up to mother's to, you know, spend some time with her, do the dutiful daughter bit, show that I cared . . .'

'Even though you didn't invite her to your dinner party.'

'Exactly. And I took a bottle of wine to cheer her up.'

'And you took the corkscrew too.'

'Yes.'

'And now,' said Russell perceptively, 'you don't want to go upstairs to ask for it, because you don't want to be beholden to her.'

Sarah, her hands still on the upturned mould, smiled. 'You understand me very well.'

'You're exactly like Bob in many ways, Sarah.'

'Ah.' A little stab of guilt. 'Has he forgiven me? How is he spending the evening?'

'Curled up with a good book.'

'Oh well, that's nice.'

'Yes. I gave him that volume of Foxe's *Book of Martyrs*.' A little turn of the knife in the wound made by the first stab of guilt. But Russell was not really vindictive. He left it at that, and went on, 'Anyway, here we are with six bottles of wine and no corkscrew. Many people would regard that as an emergency.'

Sarah agreed.

'So what are we going to do?' Russell demanded. 'I'll go out and buy one if you like. But it does seem a bit daft to do that when you've got one on the premises.'

Again, she had to agree.

'So swallow your pride, Sarah, and go and ask.'

'Yes.' She looked at him pitifully. 'I can't. Will you do it for me?'

Russell exhaled a long-suffering sigh. 'All right.'

'Just nip down and ask Clare if we can borrow hers.'

'Clare? But I thought –'

'Please.'

'Very well,' he said with another sigh.

'I'd do it myself, but with this mould . . .'

'Oh yes. Of course.' He sounded disbelieving, but he did go, leaving the kitchen door open behind him.

Sarah readdressed her attention to the Charlotte Malakoff. Holding the plate and mould firmly together, she gave it an exploratory shake. Sometimes you could hear a slight slopping which indicated it had come loose. She heard nothing, but put the dish down on the work surface and inserted one fingernail under the edge of the mould.

'Oh, I hope it hasn't broken, dear.'

The voice was so close behind her Sarah felt as if she must have leapt a foot in the air.

'Mother! You gave me a jump, creeping up like that.'

'I don't creep,' Eleanor corrected her. 'I just do not make gratuitous noise when I move.'

'No. Well, it comes to the same thing.'

Eleanor moved along the work surface away from her daughter. 'I think it's just as well, you know, Sarah, that I'm not coming to your dinner party this evening . . .'

What, was it possible that Eleanor was finally listening to the voice of reason? Could rivers flow uphill?

That the answer to both questions remained no was quickly confirmed as she went on, '. . . if you really are going to serve all that garlic.' She indicated the prawns, ready to be heated in their dishes of garlic butter.

'Mother,' said Sarah, the fate of whose Charlotte Malakoff was still unknown, 'I have got quite a lot to do, so if you don't mind –'

'I didn't come down just to be a nuisance,' Eleanor interrupted righteously. 'I just thought you might need this.'

She held Sarah's corkscrew out towards her.

'Ah. Thank you.'

'I assume you will be drinking at this dinner party of yours.'

'Yes. I would think that's not beyond the realms of possibility.'

'No, I'm sure it isn't.' Eleanor sniffed and moved towards the door. 'Well, having delivered the corkscrew, I will get out of your way and go back up to my little flat and my boiled egg.' She paused for a moment over the meat laid out on a chopping board. 'That steak looks very nice.' Then, with a 'Have a good evening, Sarah', she passed through the door.

'Thank you. Er, Mother . . .'

Eleanor stopped. 'Yes, dear?'

'What are you going to do, Mother?' Sarah asked haltingly.

'With my evening? Oh, don't worry about me. I'll watch the television.'

That was a relief. At least now Eleanor was reconciled to the situation. 'Something good on?' asked Sarah brightly.

'I believe there's a European soccer semi-final.'

'But you hate football.'

Mother gave daughter a strained smile. 'Needs must when the devil drives, Sarah,' she said, and wafted gently upstairs.

Fuming, Sarah slammed her Charlotte Malakoff down on the work surface.

She gasped when she realized what she had done. Oh no.

Gingerly, she lifted the mould. It revealed a perfect dome of almond cream and sponge fingers. It had worked.

She almost hugged herself. The Charlotte Malakoff had been a success. Maybe that would be an omen for the rest of the evening.

Chapter 18

The Dinner Party

It wasn't.

In fact, if Sarah had been looking for an omen to set the tone of the evening, a raven dripping blood on to a toad during a thunderstorm might have been more appropriate.

The minute Clifford and Gwen arrived, Sarah's memory was unlocked and she remembered precisely how much she had always disliked them. Well, to be more accurate, disliked Clifford. Gwen was such a shadowy little presence that it was hard enough to keep reminding oneself she was there, let alone feeling any emotion for or against her.

It was equally impossible to have no feelings about Clifford. He was very loud and Welsh. What Sarah had remembered as a 'forthright' manner was in reality plonking, pontificating, small-minded bigotry.

With foreboding, Sarah let them in and hung up their coats. And with mounting foreboding, she ushered them into the sitting-room and introduced them to Russell. Then, by prearrangement, she asked him to organize drinks, while she whisked off to collect some dishes of nibbles from the kitchen.

It was perhaps as well that she was out of the room for the exchange that followed, an exchange which was to set the pattern for the evening.

'Well, now, what can I get you?' asked Russell. 'Gin, whisky, sherry, Campari . . .?'

'Campari,' Clifford repeated on a gale of laughter. 'Ooh la la!'

'I beg your pardon?' said Russell.

'Campari. *Camp*ari.' Clifford explained his joke. 'Always think it sounds like a poof's drink. You should see the people who drink it too!' He laughed again at this Wildean shaft of wit.

'Do I gather,' asked Russell, 'that you wouldn't like a Campari?'

'I should coco,' said Clifford.

Russell misunderstood deliberately. 'You mean you'd like cocoa?'

'No,' Clifford replied in some bewilderment. 'I like the hard stuff. I'm a whisky man.'

'Are you?' commented Russell drily, before turning to the almost transparent figure at Clifford's side. 'Gwen, what can I get for you?'

'Something soft.'

'Surprise, surprise,' Russell murmured, as he turned to the drinks tray.

The clinking of bottles, glasses and ice sounded obscenely

loud in the silence which had crystallized in the room. Russell poured out the whisky, a bitter lemon, a dry sherry for Sarah and something for himself. Then he handed the guests their drinks and sat down with his own. There were murmurs of 'Cheers' and in the enduring silence, their discreet sips at the drinks sounded as intrusive as the clinking had.

Sarah bustled in with dishes of Twiglets, nuts and those Japanese seaweedy things which look great but taste like blotting paper.

'Goodness me,' she said breezily. 'Must be twenty past or twenty to.'

'Sorry?' said Clifford.

'An angel passing overhead.'

But this reference meant no more to him than the previous one.

'Not with you.'

'I mean nobody's talking.'

'Oh.'

Sarah looked hopefully round the room. There must be something there to prompt a comment. Surely they couldn't have run out of conversation so quickly? Drowning, she clutched at the unfamiliar liquid in her employer's glass.

'Russell,' she chuckled, 'I've never seen you drink Campari before.'

'No,' he said coldly. 'Sometimes I just feel the need.'

'Oh. Oh.' Sarah grinned around the room. Gwen reciprocated with a watery smile. Sarah let out a little, little laugh. 'Well, this is jolly, isn't it?'

The only safe subject they could find – and that took a lot of searching and a few false starts – was Clifford's work. The result was not so much a conversation as a monologue, as he expounded his views on the place of medicine in society. But at least it filled the silence, got them through the preprandial drinks, the prawns in garlic and well into the steak. And Sarah had put Vivaldi's 'Four Seasons' on low in the background to caulk any cracks that might remain.

'You see,' Clifford dogmatized, 'what is wrong with the so-called "caring" professions in this country is that they just don't care. Goodness, as a hospital administrator, I see it every day. Don't I, Gwen?'

'Yes, Clifford,' his wife whispered, for the hundredth time that evening (no doubt her lifetime total ran into millions).

'There are a large number of patients in our wards who shouldn't even be in hospital.' Clifford raised his empty glass. 'Is there some more of that wine, Russell?'

'Yes.'

'Well, don't keep it all to yourself, old boy – pass it down.' Wordlessly, Russell did as he was instructed, while the lecture continued. 'And I blame the doctors. Sheer bloody lack of imagination. Isn't it, Gwen?'

'Yes, Clifford.'

Her husband filled up his wine glass, but did not let that stop his flow. 'They get a patient they don't know what to do with and all they can think of is to shove him in bloody hospital.' He rounded on Sarah as if she had been denying this. 'It's true. You can't deny it, Sarah, it's true!'

'Well –' was the only syllable she was allowed to get out.

'Come on – what have you got to say for yourself?'

'Why should I have anything to say for myself?' she riposted with some spirit.

'Henry was a doctor,' asserted Clifford, as if that explained everything.

In fact, it just made Sarah angry. 'Clifford,' she said, with difficulty keeping on the right side of politeness, 'my being a doctor's widow doesn't automatically make me responsible for every shortcoming of the National Health Service.'

But it was not his style to let anything anyone else said

deflect the course of his argument. 'I mean, take the elderly. Hospital wards are cluttered up with elderly people who just shouldn't be there. But there's nowhere else for them. Our "caring" society has proved inadequate to the problem.'

Russell cleared his throat and made a genuine effort to contribute to the conversation. Thank you, thought Sarah. I'm going to have to spend a long time apologizing to you for this evening. 'What do you think should happen to them?' he asked.

'They should be cared for in the family,' Clifford replied, as if it had been an unbelievably stupid question, 'that's what should happen to them. That's what used to happen. They should live with their family, be cared for by their family, be included in all the family activities. Don't you agree, Sarah?'

'Well, er, yes.' This was getting a bit close to home for comfort. She felt a pang of guilt about Eleanor. 'To an extent. Do Gwen and your parents live with you?'

Clifford dismissed the idea briskly. 'No, mine are both dead and Gwen's are utterly repellent. Aren't they, Gwen?'

Like Sarah a few minutes before, 'Well –' was all she managed to say. But it sounded strange. It was not just a word, it was the subterranean rustle of a worm turning.

However, it wasn't allowed to turn far. Treading firmly on the embryonic rebellion, Clifford continued, 'Yes, so it wouldn't work in our case, but I'm talking about the principle.'

Maybe there was a half-cue there for Sarah to get a word in, but she wasn't quick enough.

'I mean, just imagine the sense of alienation an old person must feel, left out on their own, when they know that the younger generation's having a good time.'

'Yes,' Sarah agreed weakly, again uncomfortably aware of the topical relevance of his remarks.

'Your parents still around, are they, Sarah?'

'My mother is.'

'Live near?'

'Pretty near,' she confessed.

'Good. And you see a lot of her?'

'Quite a lot.'

'Excellent,' said Clifford. 'And I dare say she's included in all the family's activities?'

'Well, er . . . Some of them. Yes,' Sarah replied miserably.

Clifford's monologue continued, unrelenting, through the sweet. So unrelenting was it, in fact, that there was no opportunity for anyone to comment on the perfect appearance of the Charlotte Malakoff aux Fraises. Sarah answered the few direct questions flung at her, Gwen added to her lifetime total of 'Yes, Clifford's', and Russell made a few attempts to be pleasant. But these attempts grew farther and farther apart and ceased completely when Clifford's personal tour of the world of medicine reached the subject of AIDS, which he, somewhat outdatedly, regarded as God's punishment for the obscene crime of homosexuality.

Russell did not respond, but he was clearly finding the situation impossibly difficult, as he spelled out to Sarah when they both escaped to the kitchen to make coffee. 'I'm sorry. I really am trying, but I do just find him repulsive.'

'Yes. I'd forgotten quite how awful he was.'

'Why on earth did you invite them?'

'I don't know.' And she really didn't. There must have been reasons, there really must, but at that moment she couldn't summon up a single shred of any of them. 'The principle of reciprocal entertainment, paying people back . . .?' she hazarded. 'I suppose it's also because they're difficult. I haven't done much entertaining since Henry died, and I wanted to prove to myself that I still could. I suppose I reckoned if I was strong enough to cope with Clifford and Gwen, then I was strong enough to cope with anything.'

Russell shook his head reprovingly. 'Entertaining shouldn't be a test of strength. You shouldn't use guests like chest-expanders. Entertaining should be fun.'

'I know. I feel very contrite. Particularly for having involved you. Are you surviving?'

'Yes. Just. But I don't know how much longer I'm going to survive without punching Clifford's teeth in.'

'Oh dear.'

'I'm sorry, but he's exactly the sort of person who gets right up my nose. And if he starts displaying more of his ignorance about AIDS, I won't be responsible for my actions.'

'I don't think he's getting at you, Russell. I don't think he's realized that you –'

'That's not the point. Oh, I'm sorry, Sarah. It wouldn't be so bad if there were a few other people around to dilute him. Anyone. It only needs one more person to shift the emphasis a bit. Because I'm afraid, with just the four of us and with Gwen saying nothing but "Yes, Clifford" . . .'

'Yes.' Sarah looked at the coffee-machine. She could no longer go on pretending it wasn't ready. She picked up the full jug and put it on the tray.

Then she had an idea. It was in some ways an unattractive idea, but if there was a serious risk of Russell and Clifford's relationship degenerating into fisticuffs, anything was worth trying to salvage the evening. 'There is one thing we could do . . .' she began tentatively.

'What?'

'And I think we may be reduced to it . . .'

He looked at her quizzically. Sarah made the decision. 'Russell, would you mind going upstairs to my mother's flat and asking if she'd like to join us for coffee?'

She thought she'd probably done the right thing. The introduction of another person – even if it was her mother – must surely cause a shift in the conversation. It must surely keep Clifford away from AIDS and push him back towards caring for the elderly in the home environment. Sarah was slightly nervous about what Eleanor might have to say on that subject, but it was a risk she had to take to salvage something from the evening.

As she poured the coffee, Clifford was, needless to say, still talking, and in fact moving the conversation conveniently in the direction Sarah wanted. 'I come across absolutely pathetic cases every day. These poor old dears on the wards, utterly bewildered. It's no surpise that the suicide rate among the elderly is mounting. Is it, Gwen?'

His wife proved she was listening by varying her response to a 'No, Clifford.'

Sarah took the opportunity to speak. 'I hope you won't mind if my mother comes to join us for coffee. As I say, she lives nearby and I did ask her if she might like to drop in later,' she lied.

'Oh no, we'd be delighted, wouldn't we, Gwen?'

Gwen reverted to her traditional response.

'Now, that, Sarah, is exactly how the elderly should be treated. Made to feel part of things. I'm sure your mother really appreciates the care you show for her.'

Sarah was caught by an unexpected frog in her throat. 'Well, er, sort of.'

'I mean, I come across cases that are so tragic. Elderly people wandering round the streets because they haven't got anywhere to go – or at least nowhere to go where anyone cares for them.'

'Yes, well, I hope that –'

Sarah was interrupted by the appearance of Russell in the doorway. He had a strange expression on his face. 'Erm, Sarah,' he said over-casually, 'could I just have a word a minute?' And he beckoned with his finger.

He nodded, embarrassed.

'Well, er . . .' She flashed a smile at her guests, ignoring the surprise on their faces. 'You will excuse me a moment . . .'

When she was in the hall, Russell closed the sitting-room door and hissed, 'She's not there.'

'Mother?'

'Yes. She's not in her flat.'

'What?'

'The door's ajar, the television's on, and there's no sign of her.'

'Oh, my God,' said Sarah, as awful visions prompted by Clifford's recent words flooded into her mind.

There are some guests who tacitly recognize when an evening isn't a great success, and leave after the minimum politeness of one cup of coffee; there are others who, apparently impervious to atmosphere, stay. Clifford and Gwen were stayers. And Clifford seemed to have an inexhaustible stock of further things to say about the British Health Service.

Sarah found it hard to concentrate. Worry about where the owner of the flat above could be was now compounded by worry about what was happening in the flat below. In the agonies of her evening, she had forgotten about Clare's party, but the mounting sound of pop music left her in no doubt that it was now getting under way. Sarah unobtrusively turned up the 'Four Seasons', but Vivaldi was fighting a losing battle against Iron Maiden.

She heard Clifford saying, 'And you take my word for it, I know what I'm talking about.'

Sarah hadn't a clue what he was talking about, but since for once Gwen supplied no reaction, she felt obliged to say, 'Yes. Yes, of course.'

'Where on earth's your friend Russell now?' asked Clifford suddenly.

'Oh, he just . . . nipped out to do something for me.'

'Very obliging fellow.'

Was she being hypersensitive to detect a slight snideness in Clifford's observation, perhaps a hint that he suspected Russell's sexual orientation? She thought she probably wasn't. 'Yes. He is.'

'Are you still expecting your mother to drop in?'

Sarah laughed lightly. 'Ah. Well. Who can say? She's a very independent lady.'

'That's good. That's what one likes to hear about old people, isn't it, Gwen?'

'Yes, Clifford.'

He laughed raucously. 'No worries about your mother wandering around the streets, eh?'

Sarah tried another little laugh, which was not wholly successful. 'No. No.'

At that moment the telephone rang. She snatched it up instantly. 'Yes?'

It was Russell.

'Any sign?'

'No,' he replied. 'I've looked in all the local pubs. She's not in any of them.'

'Oh dear.'

'Shall I come back to the delights of the appalling Clifford and Gwen . . .' Sarah beamed at her guests, hoping they couldn't hear the other end of the conversation '. . . or do you want me to look anywhere else?'

'Erm.' Sarah gulped. 'Would you mind just checking the bus shelters . . .?'

She put the phone down on Russell's incredulous echo of '*Bus shelters*!'

Sarah looked up into the quizzical gaze of Clifford and Gwen. 'Sorry about that. Just, er, someone about, er, something. On the phone. Wanted to ring me about it. About something.' In desperation, she reached for the brandy bottle. 'Have a little more, Clifford?'

He accepted, thus prolonging the evening further. 'Gather you've converted the basement into a flat, Sarah.'

'Oh, er, yes.'

'Mm. Must be hard to make ends meet on a widow's pension.'

'That's not really the reason why I –'

'Young people?' Clifford interrupted.

'Sorry?'

'In the flat.'

'Oh yes. Well, a young person. Actually, it's –'

But he interrupted again before she could get Clare's name out. 'They're making a terrible racket down there.'

This was true. People who knew about such things (amongst whom Sarah did not number herself) would have recognized that what was now being played was Europe, against whom Vivaldi fared no better than he had against Iron Maiden. And even people who didn't know about such things would have recognized that the volume had been turned up.

'It's a flat-warming party,' she explained.

'That's no excuse,' Clifford stormed, moving on to a whole new set of prejudices. 'I think that generation's just bloody selfish. Their music's a symptom of it. The way they belt it out at full volume without a thought for anyone else.'

'Well . . .'

'I blame the parents,' Clifford raged on.

'Oh.'

'Don't you agree? Come on, don't you agree?'

This was a rather difficult question for her to answer. 'Well, er . . . It's a point of view, certainly. Perhaps I should explain that in fact –'

But another tweak had been given to the volume knob,

driving Clifford to fury. 'No, this is too bloody much! I think you ought to go down and have a word with them.'

Sarah tried to gloss it over. 'Oh, I don't really think that's necessary.'

'I do.'

'No. Surely –'

Clifford raised a large hand to silence her. 'I see. Yes, I fully understand. You don't think it's a woman's place to go down and complain.'

Sarah seized the let-out with relief. 'Exactly.'

'I agree with you,' said Clifford.

'Oh, good.'

'So I'll go.'

'No, Clifford. Don't –'

But her remonstrance came too late. He was across the room and out of the door before she could stop him. She heard the front door open and close.

'Oh no.'

Gwen looked across at her ruefully. 'It's no use, Sarah. Clifford's Clifford and there's no way you can change him.'

'No.'

Gwen's next line was delivered with all the accumulated bile of twenty years of marriage. 'And God knows I've tried.'

Europe were even louder when Clifford reached Clare's front door. She had not yet had a knocker put on it, so he thumped on the wood.

'Come on, come on!' he raged. 'What do you think you're playing at, you noisy little punks?'

This produced no reaction. He pounded the door again.

'Open up! Come on, or I'll complain to the police about the noise!'

Still nothing, so he started furiously hammering away with both hands.

'Look, I know there's someone in there!'

Suddenly the music cut out, leaving only his shouting and banging on the door to shatter the silence.

'Now will you just open up! Or I'll bloody well –'

The door opened. He almost fell inside, then drew back in surprise. 'Ah, good evening,' he said, confused.

'And may I ask what on earth you were making all that noise for?' asked Eleanor with icy dignity.

Chapter 19

Hangovers

It was half-past nine when Sarah, swathed in a dressing-gown, crept into her kitchen the next morning. She was heavily hungover. In part, it was an alcoholic hangover; but more, it was an emotional hangover, the aftermath of the ghastliness of the night before.

In a way, she knew, she needn't worry. So far as the Davieses were concerned, it had been a great evening. Clifford had returned from his foray to Clare's flat without commenting on what had happened, but he said nothing more about the music downstairs for the rest of the evening. And when he and Gwen eventually left, at half-past one, they had been fulsome in their assertions of what a good time they'd had. 'Haven't enjoyed ourselves so much for years,' Clifford had said, 'have we, Gwen?'

'No, Clifford,' Gwen had agreed.

Sarah's uncharitable reaction had been that this might well be true, because no one who had ever met Clifford would have made the mistake of inviting the Davieses out more than once, and so their last such social engagement had probably been years before.

Her worries about Eleanor had also been allayed when, at a quarter to twelve, she had slipped up to the flat and found the old lady in bed, snoring her head off. Sarah had no idea where her mother had been, but at least she had come back and appeared to be none the worse for her disappearance.

It wasn't the Davieses or Eleanor she was worried about, though; her guilty hangover arose from what she had put Russell through. He had returned from his abortive tour of the town's bus shelters at about midnight and then nobly put up with another hour and a half of Clifford, after which Sarah had felt obliged to feed him recuperative brandy and mollify him with abject apology.

But she still felt bad about it in the morning, and that feeling added to her general fragility.

With shaking fingers she reloaded the coffee-machine, set it going and looked round at the debris of the night before. She had shoved one load in the dishwasher before going to bed, but all the messy, awkward things – prawn dishes full of congealed garlic butter, mustard-encrusted steak plates, saucepans beribboned with clinging shreds of vegetable – remained to reproach her.

Ugh. All that effort. Even producing a perfect Charlotte Malakoff aux Fraises. And to waste it on people like Clifford and Gwen.

She slumped into a chair. She would clear up soon. But not before she'd had some coffee.

The door opened slowly and Clare, towelling dressing-gown belted tightly round her, dragged into the kitchen. She looked like Sarah felt. In fact, Sarah didn't feel quite as bad as Clare looked, which was, in a rather negative way, encouraging.

Her daughter slumped into another chair, sniffed appreciatively, pointed at the coffee-machine and mumbled, 'I've run out. They drank it all last night.'

Sarah nodded carefully, avoiding violent movements. 'Alive?' she asked.

Clare flopped forward on to the table, with her head on her crossed arms. 'Hard to say. Hungover.'

'I have the same problem. Spent a long time massaging Russell's bruised ego with brandy after the others had gone.'

This conversational flurry exhausted them for a while, and it was not until both had cups of coffee in their hands that speech again seemed possible.

'Flat-warming went all right, though, did it?'

Clare groaned. 'Well, I reckon some of the others must have worse hangovers than I've got this morning.' She winced at the pain which this long sentence caused her brain. 'Hard though that is to believe.'

'Still, probably a mark of success,' said Sarah.

'Hmm. Was yours OK?'

'No, Clare, I wouldn't really say it was. Oh, I must ring Russell. I still feel terribly guilty about him. I was just using him, not thinking. I should have realized he and Clifford wouldn't hit it off.'

'You mean they didn't?'

'You've always had a gift for understatement, Clare.' She took another blissful swallow of coffee. 'No, no, I wouldn't say last night goes down in the annals of the great social evenings. In fact it makes the Macbeths' banquet look pretty convivial.'

'Sorry,' Clare mumbled sympathetically.

A recollection came to Sarah of one of the things that had contributed to her disastrous evening. 'It wasn't just the company, actually. There were also . . . external factors. In fact, Clare, I have a bone to pick with you about the external factors.'

'Mummy . . .' Clare pleaded. 'My bones are too fragile to cope with picking at the moment.'

'No, I must say it. It's about the music. You did promise me that you'd keep the volume down.'

'But it wasn't me who kept turning it up.'

'Clare, it was *your* party. You should be able to control your friends.'

'But it wasn't any of –'

She was interrupted by the entrance of Eleanor, looking miraculously *soignée* for a Saturday morning.

She took in the two slumped figures at the kitchen table in a magisterial gaze, and greeted them with a horribly hearty 'Good morning. I was just off to the shops. Anything I can get for either of you?'

'Morning, Mother,' Sarah muttered. 'No, I don't think so.'

'Clare?'

Her granddaughter shook her head and then clutched at it. Eleanor beamed at her. 'Thank you so much for the party last night, Clare.' Sarah's head jerked up at this. 'It was very sweet of you to include me. Wasn't it a charming thought, Sarah?'

'Oh. Yes. Charming,' replied Sarah, as the pieces of the jigsaw clunked into place.

'I thought your friend with the pink hair and the earrings was most entertaining,' Eleanor went on.

'Gary.'

'Yes.' Eleanor giggled. 'Must learn to keep his hands to himself, though. Got rather fresh later on.'

Clare apologized for her guest's behaviour.

'Oh, it didn't matter,' said her grandmother roguishly.

'So you had a good time?' Sarah asked, with considerable edge to her voice.

'Splendid, yes, thank you.'

'You might have told me that Clare had invited you.'

Eleanor shrugged the idea away. 'Oh, I didn't think that you'd want to be bothered with boring details about me. Anyway, Clare didn't *invite* me to the party – she just let me know that it was likely to happen.'

Sarah nodded wryly. 'Of course. I'm surprised you could hear yourself think with the noise that was going on down there.'

'Ah, now, Sarah,' Eleanor teased, 'you must keep up with the times. I mean, nobody wants to have Iron Maiden or Europe on so's you can't hear them, do they? You can have Vivaldi murmuring away in the background if you like, but modern music is produced specifically with a view to being played at high volume.'

'Maybe, but –'

'Also . . .' Eleanor's voice took on a sudden colouring of frailty, 'you have to remember that I'm getting rather deaf. That's why I had to keep turning it up.'

'*You* were doing it?' Sarah sat up straight and tried to catch her mother's eye. Every detail was now clear. 'Of course. And you were doing it on purpose, weren't you?'

Eleanor looked at her with a vague smile. 'Sorry, dear? Didn't catch that. As I say, getting a little deaf.'

'Never mind,' Sarah growled.

Eleanor rubbed her hands together, brisker and heartier than ever. 'Well, must be off. Time and tide wait for no man.' She moved towards the door. 'I'll see you later, dear. When you're feeling better.'

'Yes.' Sarah slumped back on to the table and whispered across it, 'My God, Clare, she's got a bloody nerve!'

'Sarah,' her 'deaf' mother called from half-way across the hall.

'Yes?'

'There's no need to swear.'

Chapter 20

Christmas is Coming

The distractions of the last couple of months, getting Clare's flat organized, dealing with the awfulness of Clifford and Gwen, had enabled Sarah almost to ignore the approach of Christmas. Of course, she couldn't be completely unaware of it. Every time she went shopping, more packages had sprouted robins, bells and sprigs of holly; more windows were obscured with artificial white frosting; and more customers strutted around in short-tempered desperation trying to find 'the right thing' for unloved relations. Increasingly the interstices between television programmes were filled with tasteless cartoon trailers which promised impossibly lavish feasts of entertainment for the festive season. And the morning mail began to yield a trickle of cards from friends abroad or swots in this country who had the nerve to get that kind of thing organized before the end of November.

But, in spite of all these prompts and reminders, for a long time Sarah managed to keep Christmas at bay, just as a looming threat somewhere in the back of her consciousness. The fact that she had broached the subject of how they should spend it to her mother and Clare gave her a kind of spurious security, as if the situation was in hand.

She knew, however, that this phoney peace couldn't last for ever. Soon she would have to raise the matter again, and positive decisions would have to be made. She didn't think she could survive another Christmas with the three of them locked in together, going through the traditional routines, pretending that Henry's absence made no difference. The mould had to be broken somehow.

Perhaps one of the reasons why she was able to put Christmas from her mind so effectively for so long was her work environment. Russell made no pretence of enjoying the Season of Goodwill, and the only concession he made to it in the shop was the creation of a small section entitled 'Books to Give to People with no Detectable Interests'. Otherwise, not a sprig of holly or a single link of paper-chain was allowed to sully the customary chaos of 'Bygone Books', and customers who dared to ask, 'Do you have any books about Christmas?' were met with a glassy stare and the recommendation that they consult the 'Fairly Accessible Studies of Comparative Religion' section.

One day, early in December, Russell spelled out to Sarah (who now seemed almost fully forgiven for the Clifford and Gwen débâcle) exactly what he felt about the subject.

'I can't tell you the relief when I first admitted to myself that I couldn't stand the traditional Christmas.'

'After you met Bob?' Sarah deduced.

He nodded vigorously. 'Yes. From that moment I can date many important changes in my life – buying this bookshop for a start and . . . Anyway, the main change – the one that really encompassed all the others – was "coming out" to a new kind of honesty. I no longer pretended to like anything I really didn't like. With Christmas high on the list.

'Oh, Sarah, there is a wonderful freedom in being able to say, No, I don't actually want to foregather with all my awkward relatives for a few days of forced conviviality. I don't want to eat too much. I don't want to drink too much. I don't want to watch "The Two Ronnies". And, oh, the relief of stopping pretending I liked turkey!'

'But, however much you want to, you can't avoid Christmas completely. I mean, every time you go out, you're going to see evidence of –'

'Ah, but we don't go out.'

'So what do you do inside for all that time?'

'Decorating, usually,' he replied with a grin. 'Choose a project – this year we're going to do the hall, landing and staircase – and just get on with it. We have a complete ban on all live media, so we don't have to hear a single carol, we don't have to watch a single quizmaster dress up as Father Christmas, or see a single comedian visit a children's hospital. We just decorate and listen to the *Ring* cycle on cassette. It's bliss.'

'But what about eating? Don't you make any concessions to the season?'

Russell shook his head. 'We eat well. But we eat things we like. Things that take a lot of preparation and we don't usually have time for. Bob'll do one of his big curries. Or his Peking Duck. Heaven. The first Christmas we were together,' he recollected fondly, 'he did an entire Indonesian banquet.'

Sarah tried to imagine herself as part of that kind of scenario, but she couldn't manage it. She wanted to break the mould of a traditional Christmas, but not to that extent.

Her thoughts must have shown in her face, because Russell chuckled and said in a mocking tone, 'Oh, for you Christmas isn't Christmas without turkey and cranberry sauce and Brussels sprouts and pudding and mince pies . . .'

'And brandy butter,' she added. 'That's very important.' She sighed. 'No, Russell, you're right. I'm almost superstitious about it – feel I've missed out on some vital rite of passage into the New Year if I haven't done the full works.'

'And if you haven't spent the time with your family?'

She grimaced, but was forced to admit that that also was probably true.

'Even if they drive you to distraction?' Russell asked with a twinkle.

'Yes. Daft, isn't it?'

He shook his head in bewildered agreement. 'Absolutely crazy.'

The first week of December slipped away and Sarah didn't seem to be making much progress in her projected mould-breaking. A snowless television commercial was now a rarity, and few radio trailers went by without a background of carols. If she didn't move fast, tradition would reassert itself and the empty, painful, prickly Christmas of the last two years would be dished up again, as set in its mould as her perfect Charlotte Malakoff aux Fraises. But far less palatable.

She decided that she would sort things out over Sunday lunch. Both Eleanor and Clare had accepted the invitation to join her, and it was the obvious opportunity to talk about the threat that now loomed less than three weeks away. They couldn't be surprised when she raised the subject. After all, it had been broached before, and Sarah had got the strong impression on that occasion that Clare was as keen for change as she was. Only Eleanor needed convincing, and surely two of them could achieve that. This last thought was not entertained with total confidence. Bitter experience had taught Sarah that democracy did not play a major role in her mother's scheme of things. If Eleanor felt strongly about something, the size of the majority on the opposing side was irrelevant.

As it happened, the dreaded subject did not have to wait till Sunday lunchtime. Eleanor raised it herself when she appeared for coffee in Sarah's kitchen on the Saturday morning.

'Do you know, dear,' she said, when she was firmly entrenched at the table with a cup, 'I've just received an invitation for lunch on Boxing Day.'

This was a promising start. If they went their separate ways on one of the days, that would at least break up the solid, uncompromising wodge of holiday.

'That's nice. Who from?' asked Sarah.

'Well, you know Valerie Brown on the pension counter's sister Mary's friend, Phyllis?'

'Erm. . .' Sarah always got deeply confused when she tried to unravel the tendrils of her mother's geriatric grapevine.

'The one who does the Meals on Wheels,' said Eleanor, as if that explained everything.

'I'm not sure,' Sarah owned up. 'Do I know her? Perhaps.'

'Well, its her next-door neighbour, Frances Kettering.'

'She's the one who's invited you?'

'Yes.' Eleanor was still not confident – and with some justification – that her daughter knew who she was talking about, so provided further corroborative identification. 'Her husband's the surgeon who did Alice Grant's hysterectomy.'

'Oh.' Sarah tried to make it sound as if she now had her bearings. 'Of course.'

'Anyway, as I say, they've invited me for Boxing Day lunch. Said you and Clare would be most welcome, too.'

That might be a kind of solution. Different, anyway. No direct comparisons with Boxing Days while Henry was alive. And, in the company of strangers, surely the three of them would at least be polite to each other.

'Well, that sounds rather –'

But Sarah's sentence – and her plans – were allowed to get no further, as Eleanor interrupted, 'Of course I'll refuse.'

'Why?'

Eleanor gave a smile of pity for her daughter's slow perception, and explained, 'Well, Christmas is a family time, isn't it, dear? We just want to be the three of us together, don't we?'

'Yes,' was Sarah's automatic response. But then, thinking about it, she asked plaintively, 'Do we?'

There was also a new development from Clare's corner before the planned Sunday lunchtime confrontation. She appeared in the kitchen as Sarah was preparing supper on the Saturday evening, and came straight out with it.

'Mummy, Gary's invited me round to his place for Christmas evening.'

Good old Gary. The young man whose pink hair and earrings so intrigued Eleanor. And the precise nature of whose relationship with her granddaughter intrigued her even more.

Clare's announcement should have been good news. After all, it chimed in exactly with Sarah's mould-breaking intentions. And yet, when she heard it, she found herself suddenly depressed. There was still a kind of superstition about Christmas Day itself, and the thought of being separated from her daughter, even for part of it, left Sarah feeling as vulnerable as a peeled shrimp.

'Well, of course,' she stumbled, 'if you want to go, I'm sure your grandmother and I could . . .'

'He said his Mum wouldn't mind if you and Granny came too.'

'Oh, I don't know.' It was an appealing idea. On the other hand, knowing how Eleanor had reacted to the invitation from the Ketterings, Sarah couldn't see her mother being much more enthused by this one. 'I just feel we should be at home at Christmas and . . .'

'Oh, Mummy!' Clare snapped. 'Why, why, why? I think it should be a chance to get *out* of the home. Why is it that this great shutter comes down at Christmas? You're not allowed out to see your friends. You must stay in with the family. Christmas is just like a week of Sundays. And I've never got much goodwill left at the end of *one* Sunday spent with the family.'

'All right, Clare. You've made your point.' But it was difficult for Sarah to be angry when her daughter's opinions so closely matched her own.

Clare's voice was gentler, as she went on, 'I'm sorry, Mummy, but we can't pretend. With some things we can pretend Daddy not being here doesn't make any difference. Not with Christmas.'

'No.'

'The last two years,' Clare continued, 'we've soldiered on, bravely staying round the house, doing the traditional things and pretending it doesn't hurt. This year I don't think we should even try. I think we should take any invitation we're offered.'

Sarah nodded. 'It would certainly break the mould.'

'Yes.'

'You may be right.' Why, when Clare was so exactly echoing her own feelings, did Sarah still have a slight resistance to the idea?

'I am right, Mummy. The three of us together just get on each other's nerves. You know that. By Boxing Day we'll be at screaming pitch. If we go and see other people, at least we'll be polite to each other.'

'Yes.' Again, exactly what Sarah herself had thought.

'You never know, we might even be nice to each other.'

'Even that?' Sarah tutted at the audacity of the suggestion, then grinned at her daughter, 'Yes, I suppose we might.'

So, there was now no doubt that she had Clare on her side. Eleanor still remained to be convinced. Yes, as previously planned, that major operation would have to wait till Sunday lunchtime.

There was no doubt that things were more civilized since Clare had had her own flat, and Sunday lunch by invitation was just one symptom of this. Sarah could make her preparations in private, at her own pace, without the other two drifting in and out of the kitchen picking at the contents of her saucepans. Then, at the appointed hour, when everything was ready, they would appear for a glass of sherry. Much more civilized.

She was well ahead of herself that Sunday morning. A joint of beef was cheerfully spitting away in the oven, the vegetables were steaming gently on top, and she had time to go into the sitting-room to mop up the rest of her Christmas cards.

Clare arrived soon after twelve and they sat companionably over their sherry as Sarah scribbled away.

'Oh, no. Damn. I've done it again.'

'What?' asked Clare.

Sarah tore through a spoiled Christmas card and threw it into the wastepaper basket. 'Written "Love from Henry, Sarah and Clare".'

Her daughter's face filled with foreboding. 'Uh-uh. Here we go.'

'No, Clare, for once I am not being maudlin and self-pitying. There was no emotional trigger intended in my remark. It's just that writing Christmas cards is something I only do once a year, and after seventeen years of writing "Love from Henry, Sarah and Clare", it's a hard habit to break.'

Clare seemed to accept that.

'So. Another one wasted.' Sarah picked up a fresh card and started to write in it.

'Who were you sending my love to, anyway?' asked Clare curiously.

'Ritchie and Sandra Walker.'

'Oh no.' Clare made a face. 'Don't think I want my love sent to them.'

'Why ever not?'

'Don't like them much.'

'Oh, come on, Clare. Christmas. Season of Goodwill.'

'Yes,' her daughter agreed grudgingly. 'Goodwill to people you like. Not to people you don't like.'

'What have Ritchie and Sandra Walker ever done to upset you?'

'They gave me Arthur Mee's *History of England* for my eighth birthday,' Clare replied gnomically.

There was no answer to that, so Sarah said, 'Oh. I see. Well, I don't, actually, but . . .'

Clare rose and drifted across to look over her mother's shoulder. 'Perhaps I'd better have a look at the rest of your list and see who else you're promiscuously sending my love to.'

The list was on an old crumpled piece of file paper and dated back to many years before Henry's death. It was over-scribbled with additions, new addresses and excisions in a variety of different coloured inks.

Clare ran her finger down the names. 'Hmm. Not them. Not them. Certainly not the Higginses. Not Auntie Val.'

'But you like Auntie Val,' Sarah objected.

'Yes,' Clare agreed.

'Then why don't you want to send her a Christmas card?'

'I do. I have.'

'Ah.'

Clare explained. 'People I like I send my own Christmas cards to.'

'Oh.' Sarah's pen froze in mid-air above the next card. 'So I shouldn't be bothering to put your name on any of them?'

'No,' said Clare, drifting back to her seat.

'Just "Love from Sarah".' She wrote it and studied the effect. 'Looks a bit bleak.'

Her daughter shrugged. 'Mine just say "Love from Clare".'

'Yes, but that's different.' Sarah looked up from her task. 'You're well ahead if you've done your cards already.'

Clare nodded airily. 'I do them on the computer.'

'What computer? How?'

'At the office. I've got all my addresses stored on disc, and there's a special code for those who should get Christmas cards. I just run it through and it prints out the address labels.'

'And do the people who put their money in the building society know that it's being used to subsidize your Christmas greetings?'

'I do buy the cards,' Clare protested righteously. 'And the envelopes.'

'Oh. Just seems a bit soulless, that's all.'

'And I sign them myself,' said Clare, continuing her defence.

'Good. At least that makes them a bit more personal.' Give Clare her due, Sarah thought, her heart's in the right place.

But her daughter's next words perhaps cast doubt over this assumption. 'Well, the cards aren't standard sizes,' she said in a tone of regret. 'Don't fit in the printer.'

'Ah.' Sarah changed the subject. 'Look, when Granny comes, I do want to talk about Christmas.'

'Ugh, what a ghastly prospect,' said Clare.

'Yes, but it needn't be. I think this year —'

However, Sarah didn't get the opportunity for any more groundwork, because at that moment Eleanor arrived for her pre-lunch sherry. While Sarah was at the drinks table, her mother inspected the Christmas-card list.

'Oh, I do hope you've put my name on that card to the Potters,' she said.

'What?' Sarah handed over a glass of sherry. 'No, I haven't.'

'Why not? They're my friends, too.'

'Yes. So I thought you'd send them your own card.'

'They're not *close* friends,' Eleanor explained.

'How close do they have to be to merit an individual card?'

Eleanor sat down on the sofa and took an elegant sip of sherry before replying. 'It's very simple, dear. I have a series of lists. Close friends get a card saying "With lots of love from Eleanor". Fairly close friends get "Love from Eleanor". Male friends get "Love, Eleanor". Male friends whom I do not wish to encourage get "From Eleanor". And,' she concluded solemnly, 'the one I send to the Queen says "From Eleanor Prescott".'

Sarah darted a look across the room to stifle the beginning of a laugh from Clare. 'What, Mother?'

'Well, the Queen probably knows a lot of Eleanors.'

'Yes . . .'

'Does she ever send one back?' asked Clare, giggling ever so slightly.

'No,' her grandmother replied gravely. 'I don't put my address. Her Majesty's got quite enough on her plate without being involved in needless correspondence.'

'Very thoughtful, Granny.'

'I always try to be thoughtful, Clare.' With nobility, Eleanor turned back towards her daughter. 'And then my last list of cards are the ones that you write, Sarah.'

'That I write? What do I write?'

'You write,' her mother informed her, ' "With love from Eleanor and Sarah".'

'Oh.' Sarah took this in. 'And who are they to?'

'Well, they're to people who're more your friends than my friends, but to whom I don't wish to be uncivil.'

'I see. You'd better give me a list of them.' Sarah paused as a thought struck her. 'If they're really *my* friends rather than yours, Mother, don't you think the cards should say "With love from Sarah and Eleanor" . . .?'

Her mother shrugged and shifted the burden of blame with a deftness born of long, long practice. 'If you insist, dear. As you know, I've never been worried about petty issues of precedence.'

Sarah pursed her lips and moved to the drinks table. 'Top you up?' she asked.

When all three sherry glasses were recharged, she made her announcement. 'Listen,' she began, 'I want to talk about what we're going to do at Christmas . . .'

Chapter 21

Breaking the Mould

'So that's it, Russell. We've accepted all three.'

He looked at her in surprise, the arc of his eyebrows mirroring the curve of his half-glasses. 'Three?'

'Yes. Didn't I tell you – Wendy and Brian Sweeton have invited us for Christmas Day lunch.'

There must have been an edge of melancholy in her voice, because Russell said, 'Well, surely that's all right? You like them, don't you?'

'Yes, yes. They're lovely, but . . .'

Sarah's plans had worked. She had achieved the Christmas that she had hoped for, a social Christmas which would offer no direct comparisons with other Christmases, and yet the achievement left her strangely empty.

'*But*,' said Russell, gauging her mood correctly, 'you still feel you should be in your own home on Christmas Day, cooking your own turkey, making your own brandy butter, and so on and so on and so on . . .?'

Sarah gave an apologetic nod. 'Yes, I feel sort of dispossessed. Cheated of all those things I always complained about – fiddling with pounds and pounds of sprouts, peeling all those bloody chestnuts . . .' She sighed. 'No, I'm afraid it won't feel like Christmas if I haven't had at least one panic about the turkey breast being done but the legs still being pink inside.'

'I'm sure you're doing the right thing,' he reassured her. 'Maybe only for one year. Just to change the pattern. As you say, no comparisons.'

'Yeah.'

'Christmas must be one of the worst times,' he said gently.

'What, of bloody widowhood? You're right. There's such a public *obligation* to have a good time at Christmas, any down mood you're feeling is automatically made worse by a heavy dollop of guilt.'

'Yes, and I suppose it's a time that you and Henry were always together.'

'Actually, no.' Sarah laughed. 'I think in our entire marriage Henry and I only had one complete Christmas lunch together. That was always the trouble with being a doctor's wife. The world seemed to be crammed with pensioners staving off their heart attacks until the precise moment I got the cranberry sauce on to the table.'

Russell chuckled.

'Still, that's all gone. And this year,' Sarah continued positively, 'we are having a *social* Christmas. Lunch at the Sweetons, drop in to Gary's parents for a light snack Christmas evening, and then to Mother's gynaecologist friend for . . . I don't know . . . cold meats and salad or whatever you have on Boxing Day lunch.'

Somehow she still made the programme sound more like a sentence than a treat, so Russell observed that at least it wouldn't give her any time to think.

Sarah agreed that that was the one great advantage.

At that moment a rare event occurred.

A customer entered Bygone Books.

A meek man in his fifties, he came straight up to Russell's desk and asked if there was a section on poisons.

'Hmm. Might be something over there in "Gardening Books that are Actually Useful rather than Just a Lot of Pretty Pictures". Or you could try "Really Prurient Murder Cases" . . . Behind the glass-fronted bookcase, next to "Nonstrident Feminism".'

The customer thanked him and went off to study the shelves indicated.

'Sarah,' asked Russell in a quieter voice, 'how on earth did you get Eleanor to agree to the idea?'

'Wasn't easy.'

'I should think not. What was her reaction?'

'Appalled at first.' Sarah dropped into her imitation. '"But, Sarah, it's your *duty* to be at home and cook lunch on Christmas Day . . ." All that. And she's still very wary of the idea of going to Gary's parents.'

'Because of the pink hair and the earrings?'

'Yes, and because he's on the dole. To Mother's somewhat narrow mind, this means that his mum'll be in curlers, his dad in a grubby vest, there'll be dismantled motor-cycles all over the sitting-room, and we'll be offered greasy fish and chips out of Page Three of the *Sun*.'

'And are they like that?'

'I honestly don't know. I haven't met them. Gary himself is a nice enough lad, in spite of the hair. Talks pretty appallingly, but that doesn't mean anything these days. Even public schoolboys seem to roughen up their vowels deliberately. Street credibility is what matters.'

Russell smiled. 'I wouldn't have thought street credibility was something Eleanor has ever aspired to.'

'No. Her middle-class sensibilities are deeply threatened by the whole idea of Christmas evening *chez* Gary.'

'So how on earth have you persuaded her?'

'Actually, once we'd got all the token resistance and recrimination out of the way, it wasn't that hard. Wasn't at all hard by then.'

'Really?'

'You forget, Mother is being offered a licensed opportunity to snoop round three other people's houses.'

'Of course. Hadn't thought of that.' Russell nodded, then noticed that Sarah's expression was still rueful. 'It'll be fine. The time'll go very quickly.'

'Yes. I suppose that's the main thing.' She tried to look more cheerful, but failed. 'You know, I once met someone who claimed he went to a health farm every Christmas and had himself sedated for three days. I'm not sure that I believed him, but sometimes I can see the attraction.'

Russell made another attempt to shift her gloom. 'By this time next week it will all have happened.'

'Yes,' Sarah agreed with a trace of bitterness. 'That's the bottom line of comfort on everything, isn't it? Maybe not very positive, but it works.'

'You'll probably have a whale of a time. I'm sure they're all nice people.'

'Yes. And all bending over backwards to be extra nice to the little widow woman.'

'Don't be so cynical.'

It was a deserved reproof. Sarah knew she was being self-indulgently maudlin. But she still couldn't pretend that she was looking forward to the impending holiday, even in its revised form. 'Oh, I don't know. Partly, I don't like the idea of being on my best behaviour for two solid days. I'm sure they're all nice people, but they're not people I'm going to relax with.'

'You think you won't get a chance to let your hair down?'

'Certainly not.'

'Well, look . . .' Russell was silent for a moment, as if making a decision. 'At the end of it all, if you do want to unwind, with no pressure, just to relax . . . come round for a drink with Bob and me on Boxing Day evening.'

'Oh, thank you, Russell, but no. I don't want to interrupt your cosy wallpapering and Wagner and Peking Duck.'

'You wouldn't be interrupting anything.'

'And, anyway, I'd worry that Mother and Clare might feel a bit abandoned if I . . .'

'They'd be welcome, too . . .' He grinned '. . . if any of you are still speaking to each other.'

Sarah couldn't make a decision. Christmas was already so daunting and complicated that she couldn't see as far as Boxing Day evening. 'Well, I . . . Look, I honestly don't know what kind of state we'll be in by the end of . . .'

Russell opened his hands wide. 'Leave it completely up to you. If you want to come, come. With or without your relatives. If you don't, don't.'

'Thank you, Russell, I'm very grateful for –'

'Excuse me.'

They had been so involved in their own conversation that they had not noticed the approach of that rare visitor to Bygone Books, the customer. He was holding out a book he had found. *Poisons in Common Use around the Home.*

'Would you like that?' asked Russell.

'Please.'

Russell looked inside the cover. 'That's two-fifty then.'

The customer handed the money across and Russell put

the book in a brown paper bag, observing, 'It's supposed to be very good.'

'Yes,' said the customer. 'It's a Christmas present for my mother-in-law.'

For the rest of the week running up to Christmas, Sarah still felt empty and disorientated. There was something that kept niggling away at her.

Eventually, after much vacillation, on the afternoon of Christmas Eve she went out shopping.

And, though she knew it was silly, when she got back home, she felt a bit better.

Chapter 22

Eat, Drink . . . and be Merry?

It had arrived. They had made it to Christmas Day. Not only that, they had made it to the afternoon of Christmas Day. It was nearly quarter to seven when the three of them staggered from Sarah's Renault 4 to the front door after lunch at the Sweetons'. In the hall they all paused for breath.

'Goodness me.' Sarah, leaning back against the door frame, spoke for all of them.

'Yes,' Eleanor agreed, supporting herself against the banister. 'Wendy and Brian certainly know how to eat well.'

'And drink well,' said Clare, slumped against the wall by the door to her flat.

Sarah smacked her lips. 'That pudding was beautiful.'

Clare nodded. 'Mmm. And I don't know what that stuffing was in the turkey, but it was really yummy.'

'Yes . . .'

'And then having Stilton and nuts and port and – gosh, I feel like a barrage balloon.' It was now Clare's turn to speak for all of them. The other two nodded, winded by excess.

'Well,' said Sarah, 'at least none of us can complain that we haven't had a full traditional English Christmas Dinner.'

'No,' Clare agreed. 'We had the works.'

'Yes.' Eleanor was silent for a moment. 'Of course, it never feels quite the same when you're not on your home ground. I mean –'

'Mother . . .' Sarah raised a finger of warning. So far the day had been good. They had exchanged presents amiably in the morning and, as anticipated, being among strangers had kept them from family arguments. Sarah didn't want that record to be spoiled the minute they were alone together.

Eleanor took the point. 'Yes, dear.' She stifled the most ladylike of yawns with the back of her hand and took a couple of steps up the stairs. 'Well, I think after all that, I really must have a little lie-down.'

Clare looked at her watch. 'We're due at Gary's in three quarters of an hour.'

'Goodness, is it as late as that?' Sarah looked at her own watch for confirmation.

'Oh yes,' said Eleanor, with a little wrinkle of distaste. 'Gary's.'

'Mother, if you don't want to come . . .'

'I didn't say I didn't want to come, Sarah.'

'No, but I'm sure Gary's parents would understand if . . .'

Clare endorsed this opinion, with perhaps a little too much enthusiasm. 'Of course they would. If you're tired, Granny . . . I mean, I know you haven't *really* wanted to come from the start.'

'Have I said that, Clare?' her grandmother demanded imperiously.

'Well, not in so many words, but . . .'

'I have accepted the invitation,' Eleanor announced, as if this put an end to any possibility of second thoughts.

'Yes, but, Granny, if you're feeling a bit –'

'It would be extremely ill-mannered not to go.'

'I'm sure they wouldn't mind,' said Clare.

Eleanor rounded on her sharply. 'What do you mean?'

'Nothing.'

Sarah decided to put her oar in. 'Look, Mother, if you don't –'

But she too was overruled. 'No. I will go. I'm sure it'll be very illuminating to see how the other half lives.'

'Yes, Granny,' said Clare. And was Sarah being oversuspicious to detect the hint of a giggle in her daughter's voice?

There was a long, long silence as Sarah's Renault 4 drew away from Gary's parents' house. And, had anyone been able to see in the darkness, they would have observed a slight smile on Sarah's face, a broad grin on Clare's, and Eleanor's lips drawn tight into a thin line of pique.

She it was who eventually broke the silence. 'Well, Clare, I may say I think it was very unkind of you not to tell me that Gary's father was a knight.'

'Why?' her granddaughter asked ingenuously. 'What difference would it have made?'

'I don't know.' Eleanor pondered the question. 'I might have . . . perhaps worn a little more jewellery. Anyway,' she insisted, 'you should have told me.'

'Sorry, Granny,' Clare apologized, and then seemed to be surprised by a fit of coughing.

Sarah suddenly suffered from the same tickling in her throat, and had to jerk round the steering-wheel as the car strayed kerbwards.

'Are you sure you're all right to drive, Sarah dear?' Eleanor asked, her voice heavy with disapproval.

'Yes. Yes. Quite all right, thank you, Mother.'

Once again all was silent in the car until, with a little sigh, Eleanor said, 'The poor man, though.'

'Who?' asked Clare. 'Gary's father?'

'Yes. I mean, there he is, a man who has devoted his life to this country's exports and had his contribution publicly recognized by Her Majesty the Queen . . .' She tutted '. . . and then his son turns out to be a spunk.'

This time Clare giggled quite openly. 'I think you mean "punk", Granny.'

'I know exactly what I mean, thank you, Clare,' her grandmother snapped. 'Goodness, though, that pink hair. And he had *two* earrings in tonight.'

'Three, actually,' Clare corrected mischievously. 'He's got a little stud in the other ear, too.'

Eleanor shuddered. 'Well, it's not the sort of thing I would have expected even among the lower middle class, let alone the upper middle class. That poor, poor father. It must be such a trial for him. Don't you agree, Sarah?'

Sarah, who suddenly felt very heavy and weary, mumbled, 'Oh. Yes. Probably.'

But that wasn't good enough for her mother. 'Come on, you can be more positive than that, dear.'

'No, I can't. Not at the moment. I feel as if I'm going to burst. Clare,' she remonstrated pitifully, 'I thought you said it'd just be a light snack.'

'I thought it would be,' her daughter wailed. 'But it was nice of them to go to so much trouble.'

'Oh, yes.'

'I mean, they usually have their main Christmas meal at lunchtime, but because we were coming, they turned everything round.'

'Oh yes. I do appreciate it.' A vision of the huge plateful Gary's father had carved rose before her eyes. 'But . . . oh . . . all that turkey . . .'

'And all that pudding,' Clare groaned. 'Ooh.'

'Well,' Eleanor, who was still cross with them, observed pettishly, 'you both seemed to eat plenty of it.'

'It would have been rude not to, wouldn't it?' said Sarah. Even so, she wished at that moment that she had risked offence and eaten just a little less.

The bloated silence once again descended on them. Then Clare commented judiciously, 'Mind you, I didn't think their brandy butter was up to the Sweetons' . . .'

'No,' Sarah agreed. 'Shop-bought, I think.' Warming to the game, she went on, 'And I think if I had to cavil, the chestnut stuffing was a little dry . . .'

'Yes,' Clare picked up on the crest of a giggle, 'and the sparkling wine was rather sweet for my taste . . .'

Sarah played along. 'Oh, I agree. And I'm afraid I could only award the Christmas pudding one crossed hollyleaf . . .'

'Yes,' Clare managed to say through her giggles, 'though the £1 coins in it were a welcome change after the Sweetons' somewhat ungenerous 5ps . . .'

'And the crackers were excellent,' Sarah swept on deliriously. 'Though my companion did find the background music a little excessive. I mean, the Mormon Tabernacle Choir is an acquired taste at the best of times, but in this instance their selection of carols was hardly . . . was hardly . . .'

But no more words came out. She and Clare both broke down into gasps of giggles.

Finally, the last little ripples stopped and silence once again reigned in the car. Eleanor let it establish for a moment before rebuking them. 'Well, I think you're both extremely ungrateful. And extremely rude towards our hosts.'

'Sorry. Sorry, Mother.' Sarah was the model of contrition until another little bubble of laughter ambushed her. 'Just mildly hysterical.'

'Not hysterical, Sarah,' Eleanor contradicted. 'Ill-mannered and drunk.'

'Oh.'

'Yes. And very ungrateful.' Eleanor let the severity of this hang in the air before she observed, 'Mind you, I agree the brandy butter wasn't up to the mark . . . and my second mince pie was all pastry with hardly any filling . . . And I found the sprouts a bit soggy . . .'

Sarah didn't sleep too well that night. Partly, no doubt, this was due to the excesses of food and drink she had consumed. But, once awake, her mind filled with restlessness, a feeling that she had evaded the issue, that she hadn't had a real Christmas.

And with it came a deep sense of loss. This time it was not a complicated emotion; what she felt was very simple. She just wished that Henry was there beside her.

But the feeling was not panicky and agonizing; instead she felt a kind of calm, bone-deep melancholy.

Still, she was awake for less than an hour and in the morning felt somehow purged by the experience. If she had got through the whole holiday without thinking of Henry, it would have been another kind of betrayal.

As she sat in her kitchen on the Boxing Day morning, she looked with affection at the holes in the wall where Henry's shelf had failed. Soon she'd sort that out. Just a little Polyfilla or Tetrion and a dab of paint, wouldn't take five minutes. Yes, she'd do it. But not quite yet.

Clare joined her for coffee and said gleefully? 'See? We've got over the worst.'

'What do you mean, love?'

'Christmas Day. We've done it. It's over.'

'Yes.' A little pang of wistfulness tweaked at Sarah. 'It didn't really feel like Christmas Day.'

'That was what was good about it,' Clare assured her. 'It broke the mould.'

'Mm.'

'No direct comparisons.'

'Nope.'

'Except between different kinds of chestnut stuffing.'

'Yes.' Sarah smiled at the recollection.

'Perhaps we ought to go away next year,' Clare suggested suddenly.

'Why?' asked Sarah, alarmed at the idea.

'Again just doing something different.'

'Oh, I don't know that I could . . .' Sarah fought down the panic the suggestion had thrown her into. 'Well, next year's next year. Who knows what kind of Christmas we'll have then . . .?'

As she said it, she thought of the changes that another year might bring. Clare could have moved out by then, be married perhaps, or be in some kind of relationship . . . And Eleanor . . . well, there was always the possibility that Eleanor would not be with them in a year's time. Sarah tried to put the idea from her mind. Whatever their differences, she knew she would miss the old boot savagely when she finally did die . . .

Still, no time for gloomy introspection. She pulled herself together. 'What do you think about tonight, Clare? Do you really want to drop in to Russell's alternative Christmas?'

'Sure. Keep the variety coming. That is, assuming we survive our gynaecological lunch.'

'Hmm. And do you think Granny really wants to come to Russell's? I mean, I know she said she did, but . . .'

Clare had no doubts. 'Oh, she'll come. Now that she really will regard as seeing how the other half lives.'

'Do you think so? I can never tell whether she knows Russell's gay or not.'

'She knows.'

'Well, she always refuses to believe it when I mention the subject. Gets very cross with me.'

'She knows, Mummy. No question. And it intrigues her beyond belief. She wouldn't miss going to their house for the world.'

Sarah chuckled. 'Oh well, I'd better go and give Russell a buzz. Alert him to the invasion of three more Valkyries.'

Clare consulted her watch. 'And then it'll virtually be time to go off to the Ketterings – whoever they may be.'

'Yes, I've only met them once, incredibly briefly. It is strange,' Sarah mused, 'spending Christmas with people you hardly know.'

'Better than spending it with just the family.'

It was mildly hurtful to hear with what conviction Clare said that. But she was probably right.

'Anyway,' said Sarah briskly, 'at least we won't have to have full Christmas lunch again at the Ketterings.' She laughed. 'I mean, no one would do that on Boxing Day, would they?'

'Well, you were wrong, weren't you, Mummy?' said Clare, as the Renault 4, seemingly as sluggish and bloated as its passengers, chugged away from the Ketterings' house.

'Yes,' Sarah concurred dully. 'I was wrong.'

'It was very nice of them, though,' Eleanor observed.

'Oh yes. Very nice.' A vision of a mince pie, larded with

brandy butter, loomed in Sarah's mind. With a ferocious effort of concentration she chased it away.

'I mean,' Eleanor went on, 'to change their whole Christmas round in our honour.'

'Yes. Everyone's being very kind.'

As she spoke, the image of a turkey leg, smothered in cranberry sauce and crowned with a dollop of chestnut stuffing, swam into her consciousness. It was harder to chase that away.

'Mind you,' Clare began perkily, 'I didn't think their cranberry sauce was up to the Sweetons'. And the turkey was tougher than the one we had at Gary's. And –'

For Sarah, who had just driven the turkey leg out of her mind, this was too much. 'Please. Clare. No.'

'What?'

'Please don't talk about food. Least of all turkey. I just don't think my digestion can cope.'

'Well, we had to eat it, didn't we?' Clare argued. 'After they'd gone to all that trouble.'

'Yes. Yes. We had to. But just . . . let's not talk about it.'

Clare had the good grace to subside into silence.

It was two or three minutes later that Eleanor spoke. Her voice was distant, musing. 'You know,' she announced, 'if Alice Grant had been there, I think she would have been really reassured . . .'

'Alice Grant?' Sarah repeated, confused by this sudden *non sequitur*. 'The one who had the hysterectomy?'

'Yes.'

'Why would she have been reassured, Mother?'

Eleanor sighed dreamily. 'Did you *see* the way Mr Kettering carved that turkey?'

Chapter 23

Never the Same

Sarah replaced her teacup in its saucer and sighed with satisfaction. 'Lovely. Strange, isn't it? However full you feel, always got room for a cup of tea.'

'Oh yes. Always,' Eleanor agreed enthusiastically. They were both flopped in Sarah's sitting-room with their feet up, husbanding their dwindling energy before the next foray, out to Russell and Bob's.

'As a matter of fact, Sarah dear, even though I knew we weren't going to be home much this Christmas, I did still make my usual Christmas cake.'

Mistaking Sarah's expression of horror for one of incomprehension, Eleanor explained, 'You know, with the rough icing and the silver balls and the little tree and Father Christmas going down the slope on his sleigh. If you'd like a slice . . .' She made as if to rise '. . . I could just slip upstairs and —'

Sarah raised a languid hand to stop her. 'No, Mother. No. Really, but . . . No.'

Eleanor looked a little wistful. 'I don't know. It doesn't really feel like Christmas without a slice of Christmas cake.'

'Plenty of time, Mother. It's only Boxing Day. You forget, Christmas lasts for about a week these days.' But, she thought gleefully, we've broken the back of it. We really have broken the back of it.

'Yes.'

Eleanor looked so cast down that Sarah asked her with a smile, 'Go on, tell me – could you honestly manage a slice of Christmas cake at this precise moment?'

'Well, I don't know.' Eleanor vacillated. 'Perhaps I . . . No. No, you're right, dear. I couldn't.' But she didn't sound absolutely convinced.

At that moment Clare came into the sitting-room. On her face there was a strange expression, made up partly of accusation and partly of amusement. It was as if she was in possession of a private joke and, as yet, undecided whether or not to share it.

'Mummy?'

Sarah looked across at her wearily. 'Yes, love?'

'I've just been into the larder.'

'Oh? Surely you're not still hungry?'

'No. I opened the freezer.'

'Ah.' Sarah had a nasty feeling she knew what was about to come, but she tried to delay its arrival. 'Why?'

'I wanted to put that necklace Gary gave me into it.'

'What?'

'That Glow-in-the-Dark Disco Necklace . . .'

'Oh yes, I remember it. But why on earth in the freezer?'

'They keep their glow longer if you freeze them.'

'Do they? That's remarkable. I wonder what it is in them? What kind of chemical can it be that –'

'Mummy . . .' Clare cut across her babbling.

'Yes?'

'Stop trying to change the subject.' She looked at Sarah with a knowing grin. 'You know what I found in the freezer, don't you?'

'Well, er . . .'

Sarah's obvious discomfiture had now roused Eleanor's interest. 'What did you find, Clare dear?'

Clare ticked off the items on her fingers as she went through them. 'I found a turkey, Brussels sprouts, chestnuts, mince pies, brandy butter, Christmas pudding . . .' Again she grinned at her mother. 'Do you want me to go on?'

'No. No, that's all right. That's plenty.'

Eleanor was confused. 'I don't understand. Why is this, dear?'

'Well . . .' Sarah sighed sheepishly. But there was no way round it. She was caught, and she would have to spell out exactly what had happened. 'Christmas Eve, I . . . I don't know, I was out shopping, and I was feeling sort of . . . well, feeling that it seemed a bit sad that we weren't doing the full Christmas bit this year, and I wasn't going to get the chance to worry about the turkey breast being done and the legs still being pink inside, and I thought maybe it'd be a good idea if we had our own little Christmas lunch next Sunday . . . you know, just the three of us . . .' She felt herself wilting under their combined gaze. '. . . and I thought that maybe, you know, just a little turkey and a few Brussels sprouts and a smidgeon of chestnut stuffing and . . .' She petered out. 'As I say, I thought it might be a good idea.'

She tried to cover her embarrassment with a brave smile but the irony in the faces of her mother and daughter made her feel deeply stupid.

'Mind you,' she concluded in a small voice, 'it doesn't seem quite such a good idea now, does it?'

Russell and Bob shared a tall Edwardian house, not dissimilar to Sarah's own, on the other side of the town. The three women huddled together in the chilly porch as Sarah rang the doorbell.

'Hope they're not in the middle of decorating,' she said.

'Or anything else,' Eleanor muttered darkly.

'Mother!'

The door opened to reveal a beaming Russell. 'Wotan's Farewell' sounded from a distant cassette recorder.

'Hello. Welcome to you all. Happy Christmas.'

He ushered them into the warm. Eleanor said appropriate nice middle-class things while she gazed unashamedly around the hall. Sarah wondered what on earth her mother was expecting to see. Erotic prints? Obscene sculptures? Naked Japanese houseboys?

'This really is most kind of you. Much appreciated, Russell,' Eleanor trilled.

'No problem. Lovely to see you,' he said, helping her off with her coat.

'How's the decorating?' asked Sarah, as she removed her own.

'Fine. Done the landing and we're half-way down the stairs.' He gestured down a passage. 'Look, do go through into the kitchen. Bob's doing wonderful things in there, and I think just now he's sorting out some Black Velvet.'

'Great,' enthused Clare, who seemed to have got a second – or possibly seventh – wind. 'Come on, Granny.'

'Will I like Black Velvet?' Eleanor asked her granddaughter in a wary stage-whisper.

'Yes. Of course you will.'

'It's not a drug, is it?' Eleanor hissed through closed teeth.

Clare giggled as she led the way. 'No, Granny. It's not a drug.'

Russell did not follow them straight away. He looked at Sarah and asked gently, 'So . . . how's it been?'

'Fine.' She hesitated. 'Well . . . not the same.'

'It never will be, Sarah.'

'No.' She had always known that, but accepting it was still not easy. 'And you, Russell?'

'Terrific. This is our fourth time right through the *Ring* cycle.'

'Rather you than me.'

Suddenly Sarah was aware of a smell that was horribly, ominously familiar. She sniffed suspiciously. 'Russell, what is that?'

He gave her a knowing smile. 'Ah. That is our surprise.'

'Surprise?' she asked weakly.

'Yes, Sarah. Specially in your honour.'

'What is it, Russell?' But she knew, with terrible foreboding, what his answer was going to be.

She was, of course, right. 'Well, Sarah, you sounded so wistful before Christmas. You know, all that about missing the traditional bit, and I mentioned this to Bob and . . . well, he's taken pity on you.'

'In what way?' she asked, resigned to her fate.

'He's changed the habits of a lifetime. Specially for you, he's cooked turkey and Brussels sprouts and roast potatoes and chestnut stuffing and cranberry sauce and . . .'

'Ah,' said Sarah.

Then, like a tidal wave, the humour of the situation hit her and ripple after ripple of laughter ran through her body.

Tears streamed from her eyes and it was a few minutes before she could see anything.

When she regained the faculty of sight, she looked up into Russell's bewildered face.

'Are you all right, Sarah?'

'Yes. Yes, I will be.' Another little flurry of laughter ran through her. 'Go on through. I'll just mend my face and then I'll be with you.'

Still puzzled, Russell went off to join Bob and his other guests.

Sarah looked at her face in the hall mirror, and dabbed at her tear-stained eyes with a tissue. At least, she comforted herself, this time they're tears of laughter. That, after the last two years, is a welcome change.

Then she thought of Henry, and allowed herself a couple of quick tears of the other sort.

She blew her nose, putting that indulgence behind her, and she thought of the last few months. Things were getting better. Slowly.

Clare was in her flat. That was the biggest positive achievement.

And Sarah had learnt things about herself. Some of the learning had been painful. She thought, still with a blush, of her encounter with Nick. She remembered the emptiness of her meeting with Janie. And she still winced at the recollection of the evening with Clifford and Gwen.

But, even through all those embarrassments, there did seem to be a tiny thread of progress. Each encounter had taught her something. Each mistake was one that would not be made again.

Nothing would ever be the same, but sometimes that little

confidence returned that she could go on, that she could sort out a new life. After Henry.

With that thought, Sarah France turned from the mirror and went to join the people who infuriated her most and whom she loved most in the world.

And to eat her fourth full Christmas Dinner in two days.